"The Western genre   n
original voi

PRAISE FOR
BULLETS AND LIES

"[Talbot Roper's] not afraid to use his gun, though he'd prefer to use his brain. Eventually he works things out, but not before Randisi has provided some good surprises. Short chapters, good pacing, and a fine start to a new series. Fans of the traditional Western should get it immediately."

—Bill Crider

A rude awakening . . .

Giles and Hague drew their guns, and Giles silently indicated to Hague that he should kick the door in. Hague nodded, backed up so that he was flat against the wall, then launched himself at the door. His feet struck it just below the doorknob and the door slammed open.

There was a flash of light from inside, and a bullet struck Hague dead center in his torso.

Giles panicked and turned to run, but Dol fired twice, hitting him both times and putting him down . . .

Dol ran down the hall, just as Roper came out his door. For a moment they pointed their guns at each other, then backed off.

Berkley titles by Robert J. Randisi

BULLETS AND LIES
THE RELUCTANT PINKERTON

THE RELUCTANT PINKERTON

A Talbot Roper Novel

ROBERT J. RANDISI

BERKLEY BOOKS, NEW YORK

THE BERKLEY PUBLISHING GROUP
Published by the Penguin Group
Penguin Group (USA) Inc.
375 Hudson Street, New York, New York 10014, USA

USA I Canada I UK I Ireland I Australia I New Zealand I India I South Africa I China

Penguin Books Ltd., Registered Offices: 80 Strand, London WC2R 0RL, England
For more information about the Penguin Group, visit penguin.com.

THE RELUCTANT PINKERTON

A Berkley Book / published by arrangement with the author

Berkley Books are published by The Berkley Publishing Group.
BERKLEY® is a registered trademark of Penguin Group (USA) Inc.
The "B" design is a trademark of Penguin Group (USA) Inc.

For information, address: The Berkley Publishing Group,
a division of Penguin Group (USA) Inc.,
375 Hudson Street, New York, New York 10014.

ISBN: 978-0-425-25071-6

PUBLISHING HISTORY
Berkley mass-market edition / July 2013

PRINTED IN THE UNITED STATES OF AMERICA

10 9 8 7 6 5 4 3 2 1

Cover illustration by Dennis Lyall.
Cover design by Diana Kolsky.
Interior text design by Laura K. Corless.

This is a work of fiction. Names, characters, places, and incidents either are the product
of the author's imagination or are used fictitiously, and any resemblance to actual persons,
living or dead, business establishments, events, or locales is entirely coincidental.
The publisher does not have any control over and does not assume any responsibility for
author or third-party websites or their content.

ALWAYS LEARNING   **PEARSON**

Prologue

Talbot Roper was considered to be the best private detective in the country. That was why the town of Rockwell, Wyoming, had hired him to find out who had robbed their bank, killed the bank manager and the sheriff. He'd had a meeting with the mayor and the town council to listen to their proposition.

Rockwell was a growing town, the kind that had the fresh smell of wood in the air from the new buildings that had been erected recently. And they had a new bank, complete with guards and a new safe, which had nevertheless been robbed, and rather easily.

"I don't understand why you sent for me, gentlemen," Roper had said. "Haven't you appointed a new sheriff?"

"We have," the mayor said, "but we don't feel he's up to this job. We need someone who can find out how they were able to rob the bank, who they are, and where they went. We need someone who won't be concerned with jurisdictional questions."

"What about a bounty hunter?"

"We thought about that, but we don't know who to send

him after," the mayor said. "We understand that you have all the talents necessary to discover who the robbers were, and then to track them down."

Roper looked at the five men seated at the council table. They were all local merchants, all in their fifties or sixties, and they were all watching him intently.

"I don't come cheap, you know," he said.

"We understand that," the mayor said. "We on the council are prepared to pay your bill."

"And you're right," Roper said. "I'm a detective, I can figure out who they are and how they did the job. And I can track them. But I'm not a gunman. I won't kill them. I'll turn them over to the law."

The five men all exchanged glances, and then the mayor said, "That's fine with us."

"And I'll recover whatever money is left," Roper added.

"Agreed," the mayor said.

"All right, then," Roper said, "I'll need a retainer, and I'll submit a full bill when the job is done . . ."

It didn't take him long to do the detective work and find out that the two guards had been in cahoots with the bank robbers. They were each supposed to receive a cut of the proceeds, but instead they had both been murdered afterward. A witness to the killings had been left behind, and Roper was able to pin the whole thing—to his satisfaction—on a gang led by a man named Stu Milligan. From that point on, the job became to track down the Milligan gang.

All of which had led him to Festus, Missouri.

Festus was a small town, no scent of fresh lumber in the air, no impression of growth as he rode down the main street. There were a couple of saloons, a hotel, a general store, and a small bank. The bank certainly didn't look worth robbing, but this was where the trail led. Something had led the

Milligan gang here, months after the robbery of the bank in Rockwell.

Roper reigned in his Appaloosa in front of the sheriff's office and dismounted. He tied it off and stepped to the door. It was ajar, the lock broken. He went inside. The man behind the desk was wearing a star, but he was a match for the office, which was in disarray, and for the door—broken.

He had a bottle of whiskey in one hand and a coffee mug in the other as he looked up at Roper. The detective could see a layer of dust on almost every surface.

"Help ya?"

"You can if you're the sheriff."

The man looked down at his chest. A lock of gray hair fell down over his forehead as he did. Then he looked back up at the detective. Roper guessed him to be mid-forties, even though at first appearance he looked older.

"This tin star says I am, but it don't tell the whole story."

"I don't know if I have time for the whole story, Sheriff."

The neck of the bottle clinked against the mug as he poured himself a couple of fingers of whiskey.

"Want a drink?"

"I could use one," Roper said. "I've been riding a while."

"Mug over there on the stove."

Roper walked to the old potbellied stove, grabbed the chipped mug from the top, and carried it over. He used his bandanna to clean out the inside, not that it made it that much cleaner.

"Have a seat," the sheriff said, pouring him a drink. "What's on your mind?"

"I'm tracking a gang led by a man named Milligan."

"Ned Milligan?"

"No, Stu."

"Stu's the older," the sheriff said. "Ned's second."

"Are there more?"

"One more," the lawman said. "Terry."

"And the rest of the gang?"

"Not related. You after the whole gang?"

"I'm after the ones who robbed a bank in Rockwell, Wyoming, and killed some men, including the local sheriff."

"You track them all the way from Wyoming?"

"I have."

"Bounty hunter?"

"Detective."

"Oh? Pinkerton?"

"Once upon a time," Roper said, "but I've been on my own for a long time now."

"Hmm," the sheriff said, pouring himself another drink.

"What's your name?" Roper asked.

"Hmm? Oh." He sipped his drink first, then said, "Howard, Sheriff Tom Howard."

"Well, Sheriff Howard, I'm assuming you know the Milligans, since you know all their names."

"I've heard of them," the sheriff said. "They're from around here. I'm surprised they got as far as Wyoming."

"Well, they did," Roper said, "and they made their mark, which they're going to have to pay for. If they're from around here, then you can tell me where to find them."

"I probably could," Howard said.

Roper waited a few moments, then asked, "But will you?"

Howard looked at Rope and said, "Hmm?"

"The Milligans," Roper said. "Will you tell me where to find them?"

For a moment Roper thought the lawman had gone catatonic, but then the man shrugged and said, "Why not?"

The sheriff agreed to tell Roper where he could find the Milligans.

"But I can't go out there with you," he added.

"Why not?"

"Well, for one thing," the man said, "they ain't wanted hereabouts."

"And for another?"

In answer to that the sheriff stuck his right hand—his gun hand—out so Roper could see it shake.

"I ain't been much good lately, not for a while," the law-man said. "I'd probably just end up gettin' you killed."

"Good point," Roper said. "Don't worry about it. I'll handle it myself. Just tell me where they are."

"They're in one of two places. They're either at the house they all live in north of town, or they're in Stallworth's Saloon."

"Here in town?"

The lawman nodded.

"I didn't see it when I rode in."

"It's not on Main Street," the sheriff told him. "It's on a side street called Prescott Street."

"This town has side streets?"

"Three of 'em," Howard said. "Brown, Clinton, and Prescott Street."

"You got any deputies?"

"No. There's no money in the budget for deputies."

"For a mayor?"

"Yeah."

"Town council?"

"Sure."

"So if I do what I have to do to catch these guys, will you back me with them?"

"Do you have a warrant?"

"I don't need a warrant," Roper said. "I'm not a lawman. But there are posters out on these guys for bank robbery and murder—the murder of a lawman—in Wyoming. I intend to take them back there, dead or alive."

"How are you any different from a bounty hunter?" the lawman asked.

"I'm not after a reward," Roper said, "I'm not looking to collect a price on their heads. I'm working for a fee—I'm being paid a salary, same as you are."

"I think I get it," Howard said.

Roper stared at the man for a few moments. There was something familiar about him.

"Have we met before?" he asked.

Howard averted his eyes and said, "I don't think so."

"I think we have," Roper said. "I can't think about it now, but it'll come to me."

"When do you want to take these fellas?" Howard asked.

"As soon as I can," Roper said. "I've still got daylight to work with."

"You know what they look like?"

"I've got pretty good descriptions to go by," Roper replied, "especially of Stu."

"You'll know Terry and Ned when you see 'em," Howard said. "They look just like him."

"I've got a question," Roper said. "When I mentioned the Milligans, you immediately said Ned. Why?"

"Ned's the bad one," Thomas said. "Stu's the leader, but if somebody pulled the trigger on that lawman, it was Ned."

"You know these guys," Roper said. "I mean, *know* them, not just know of them."

"Yeah, I do," Howard admitted.

"Sheriff," Roper said. "I think you might need to help me take them in."

Howard eyed the whiskey bottle on his desk, then put the stopper back in and said, "You might be right, Mr. Roper."

Roper waited while the lawman got himself together. The man put on a new shirt that he hadn't sweat through, then strapped on his gun and donned his hat.

"Let's go," he said. "I'll show you where Stallworth's is."

"Lead the way."

As they left the office, Roper noticed the man was tall and slender, almost too thin. In profile he still thought he'd met the man before, but still couldn't place him.

Outside, Howard stopped by Roper's horse, looked at his saddle holster.

"That's a good idea," he said. "Extra gun without having to tote it around on your hip yourself."

"Yes," Roper said, "it's come in handy a time or two."

"Do you wanna leave your horse here?"

"Yes, no point in taking it over to the saloon," Roper said. He removed his rifle from its scabbard. "I'm ready."

They walked along the deserted Main Street for several blocks. There were lights in only a few of the buildings they passed, but none of them were saloons.

"Are there no saloons at all on Main Street?" Roper asked.

"That's right," Howard said. "We have three saloons, one each on the side streets."

At that moment Roper noticed they were passing Clinton Street. Down the street, to his right, he saw lights and heard some music coming from one of the saloons.

"I see," he said.

A couple of more blocks and they reached Prescott. Similarly, down the street there were lights and music.

"There it is," Howard said.

Roper started down the street, then stopped and looked back at the lawman.

"You coming?" he asked.

Howard wiped his palms on his thighs and said, "Yeah, sure."

Inside Stallworth's Saloon, Terry Milligan sat with Ben Abbott and Jack Newman, two of the men he robbed the Rockwell bank with. The other two—his brothers Stu and Ned—were not present.

Stallworth's was a working man's saloon. There was a piano in the corner, being played badly by a skinny man with a cigar in his mouth. There was no gambling offered, unless you wanted to start your own poker game. And there were no girls working the floor. You went to the bar and got your own drinks. The three men had a bottle of whiskey on the table, and Abbott was refilling their glasses.

"How long we gotta stay in this one-horse town?" he demanded.

"Hey," Terry said, "this is where I grew up. Don't be bad-mouthing Festus to me or my brothers."

"I don't think your brothers would much care," Newman said.

Terry glanced at Newman, who looked closer to his twenty-four years than any of the others. Stu, Ned, and Ben Abbott were in their thirties.

"Look," Terry said, "my brothers are coming up with new plans for us. We just gotta wait a little longer."

"Well," Abbott said, "I hope the new plans don't involve killin' any more lawmen."

"That Ned," Newman said. "He's a little crazy."

"Hey," Terry said, "watch how you talk about my brother . . . he's more than a little crazy."

The three men laughed and drank.

Roper and Howard approached the front of the saloon.

"Are they in there?" Roper asked.

Howard mounted the boardwalk and peered over the batwing doors. He returned to stand with Roper in the street.

"Terry Milligan is in there along with Ben Abbott and Jack Newman."

"Are they part of the gang?"

"Oh, yeah," Howard said. "They all rode in together a couple of weeks ago, along with Ned and Stu."

"Okay," Roper said. "Let me take a look, see if I can match them to their descriptions before I go in."

This time Roper stepped to the batwings and peered over them. There were several tables of men, and more standing at the bar. But he was able to identify Terry Milligan right away. He was one of the men with a "big head." Apparently, the Milligans shared that particular feature.

The other two men were wearing trail clothes—like Terry Milligan—and their hats were on the table. One of them was "big and floppy," according to one of the tellers. And one of the men had a "barbershop quartet" mustache and muttonchops. Roper went back to Howard.

"I've seen enough to convince me it's them," he said.

"When I take them back to Rockwell, they can be properly identified."

"Alive or dead."

"I will bring them back alive if I can," Roper said. "It would be easier—and more legal—with your help. And the reward could then go to you."

"I'm not interested in any reward," Howard said quickly, "and I don't want any credit."

"I just want to be able to say I had the law on my side," Roper replied. "Would you sign a statement saying you were with me when I apprehended them?"

For a moment he thought the lawman was going to decline, and then Howard said, "I suppose so."

"All right," Roper said. "I'm going to walk in there and try to get the drop on them. You can stay out here and watch. You don't have to get involved unless you want to."

"If you need help," Howard said, "I'll be there."

"I know you will," Roper said.

He mounted the boardwalk, and this time went inside.

Roper set his rifle down on the bar, ordered a beer, kept his eyes on the three men in the mirror behind the bar. He counted eleven other men in the place, plus the bartender, and none of them were paying him any attention.

He turned with the beer in his left hand and looked at the table with three members of the Milligan gang sitting around it. It was quiet in the place, and whatever conversations were going on were being held in low tones. When he spoke, everyone in the place would be able to hear him, but there was no way around it.

He drew his gun and said, "Terry Milligan."

"Yeah?" Milligan said. He turned his head to see who had called his name and froze when he saw the stranger holding a gun on him. "Wha—"

The other two men, Abbot and Newman, looked over at him.

"You and your friends just take it easy," Roper told them.

"What is this?" Milligan asked.

"I'm taking you in for bank robbery and murder in Wyoming."

"This ain't Wyoming," Milligan said.

"Well, we'll just go on back there," Roper said.

Milligan looked around while Abbott and Newman kept their eyes on the gun.

"Looks like you're here alone," Milligan said.

"Looks like."

"You figure on takin' my brothers back, too?"

"Oh, yes."

"All five of us? On your own? You got a lotta confidence."

"I'm holding the gun."

"There's three of us," Milligan said. "One of us'll get you."

"I'll kill one, maybe two of you with no problem," Roper said. "Who wants to go first? Look at your friends. Not them."

Milligan snuck a look at Abbott and Newman, who didn't return the look.

"Doesn't look promising, does it?" Roper asked.

Mulligan looked back at him.

"You might take us, but you won't take my brothers," Milligan said.

"We'll see. Now you and your friends drop your guns to the floor."

None of the three men moved.

Roper cocked the hammer on his gun.

Abbott and Newman took their guns out and dropped them to the floor.

"Now you, Milligan," Roper said, "unless you want to be a big man."

"What's your name?" Milligan asked.

"Roper," the detective said. "Talbot Roper."

"You're a dead man, Roper."

"We'll see," Roper said. "Now drop it, or use it."

Milligan stared at him for a few seconds, then took his gun from his holster reluctantly, and dropped it.

Roper holstered his gun and grabbed his rifle from the bar, at the same time shouting, "Sheriff!"

After Sheriff Howard and Roper put the three members of the Milligan gang in a jail cell, they stood in the office facing each other. Howard hung the key on a peg in the wall.

"Now what?" he asked.

"Now I'll go and get the other two while you stay here with these."

"You're goin' up against Ned and Stu Milligan alone?"

"Do I have a choice?"

"How fast are you with that gun?"

"I'd hate to have to depend on the answer to that question," Roper said. "I'd prefer to get the drop on them, like I did with these three."

"It might not be as easy," Howard said. "You'll have to watch Ned. He's pretty fast."

"And Stu?"

"Like I said, he's the brains, but he can hit what he shoots at."

"Okay, thanks."

Roper headed for the door.

"Hey."

"Yeah?"

For the second time Howard dried his palms on his thighs.

"I could come and back your play."

"What about these three?"

"They ain't gonna get out," Howard said.

Roper thought about it, then said, "No, that's okay. I wouldn't want to get you killed, Sheriff. You've helped me enough. You better just stay here."

He went to the door, put his hand on the knob, then it was his turn to say, "Hey."

"Yeah?"

"If I don't come back," Roper said, "you better just let these three go."

Howard grabbed his hat and jammed it on.

"I'm comin' with you."

"But—"

"If you don't come back," he said, "I'm probably a dead man anyway."

Roper thought about that, then said, "Good point."

The house the Milligan gang was living in—or "squatting in," as Sheriff Howard put it—was walking distance from town, so once again Roper took his rifle and left his horse in front of the sheriff's office.

"Maybe," Roper said, "we should check the other saloons to be sure they're not in town."

"The Milligans only drink at Stallworth's," Howard told him.

"If they're such regulars there, do you think someone told them by now that their brother and the rest of the gang are in jail?"

"It's possible, I guess," Howard said.

"In which case they know we're coming."

"They know you're comin'," Howard said. "They won't be expecting me."

"That's a good point," Roper said, "and one that we could use to our advantage."

"So then, how do you want to play it?" the lawman asked.

"There are a couple of ways we could go," Roper said. They discussed them as they continued to walk.

Inside the house, Ned and Stu Milligan were sitting at the table, drinking coffee.

"Where's Terry?" Stu asked.

"He's at Stallworth's with Abbott and Newman," Ned said.

"I wish he wouldn't drink with them," Stu said.

"Well, maybe we should tell him that we intend to cut them loose," New said.

"The hard way," Stu said, and the two men laughed.

"We pulled enough jobs with them," Ned said. "Time to let them go."

"For good!" Stu said, and they laughed again.

The inside of the house was almost bare, except for the table, the stove, and five bedrolls. It was stuffy and dirty and smelled of men's sweat.

"Jesus," Stu said, "it stinks in here. Open that door and let's air it out."

"I don't smell nothin'," Ned said.

"That's cause most of the smell is comin' from your feet."

Ned didn't reply, but got up and walked to the door.

Roper decided to go straight in.

He and Sheriff Howard reached the outskirts of the grounds around the house, where the sheriff could remain hidden behind some trees while Roper approached the house.

Just as Roper was reaching the house, the front door suddenly opened and one man appeared there. Roper stopped, caught with no place to go, and the two men stared at each other.

Damn, he thought.

Roper heard the man call to his brother Stu, which made this Ned. He was mindful of what the sheriff had told him, that it was Ned who was the gunman.

Talbot Roper was not a gunman, he was a detective. He knew how to use a gun, but he was not a fast draw. He left that to the Hickoks and Mastersons. But he had something else that served him well against faster men—he was cool, and he was accurate.

The second man joined the first at the door, and they stared at Roper.

"Hey, boys," Roper said. "Did you get the news?"

"What news?" Stu asked.

"Your brother's in jail, along with his two friends," Roper said.

"In jail?" Ned asked. "What are you talkin' about?"

"They're under arrest."

"What for?"

"Bank robbery and murder, in Wyoming."

"Frank wouldn't dare," Stu said.

"Who?" Roper asked.

"The sheriff," Stu said. "He wouldn't dare arrest them. He's got no jurisdiction."

"He didn't arrest them."

"Then who did?"

"I did."

"Who the hell are you?"

"The name's Talbot Roper."

"What the—" Ned started, but Stu stopped him, said something in his ear. Roper had the feeling Stu Milligan knew his name. After all, he was supposed to be the brains.

"Whaddaya want here?" Ned asked.

"I'm taking you two in, as well," Roper said.

"You ain't a lawman," Ned said.

"I don't have to be," Roper said. "I was hired by the town of Rockwell to bring you boys back."

"The whole town?" Stu asked.

"The whole town."

The Milligans stepped out of the doorway onto the porch and moved apart so they wouldn't be in each other's way. There had been one moment when Roper could have taken them in the doorway, when they were standing too close together, but the moment had passed.

"You got one chance, Roper," Stu said. "Right here. And after we kill you, we'll go get Terry out of the jail."

Roper kept his eyes on Ned. He would move first.

"Hold it, boys," Sheriff Howard said. "I can't let you do this."

All three men looked over at Howard, who had come from Roper's right with his gun out. He had the Milligans covered.

"Stay outta this, Frank," Stu said.

There it was again, Roper thought. Stu Milligan called the sheriff "Frank." He now knew where he had seen the man before.

"Can't do that, Stu," the lawman said. "You boys are gonna have to drop your guns."

"Let us do this," Ned said. "Us against him. It's only fair."

Sheriff "Howard" looked at Roper.

"I'm no fool," Roper said. "You've got the drop on them, Sheriff."

"We ain't droppin' our guns," Stu said, "so you're gonna have to shoot . . . Sheriff."

Roper still kept his eyes on Ned. He knew they meant what they said. They weren't giving up. The sheriff might take Stu—who was between the lawman and Ned—but Roper was going to have to take Ned.

"All right," Roper said. "Now you've got one chance, boys."

"No chance—" Ned said, and went for his gun.

Roper drew, but knew Ned had him beat. He heard the shot, felt a bullet tug at his shirtsleeve. When he fired, it was with a steady hand and great confidence. He put a bullet right in Ned's chest before the man could fire again.

He was aware of the other shots, but dared not take his eyes from Ned until the man hit the ground. When he did look, Stu Milligan was also facedown on the porch.

The sheriff walked over and stood next to him.

"You got nicked," the man said, looking at Roper's arm.

"It's not bad," Roper said. He replaced the spent shell in his gun and holstered it.

"I'd better get somebody out here to collect the bodies," the sheriff said. "You gonna want to take them back?"

"The live ones will be good enough," Roper said. "You got a potter's field?"

"We do."

"Put them in there."

The lawman nodded, and they started walking back.

* * *

The next morning Roper came into the sheriff's office to collect his prisoners.

"Coffee?" the sheriff asked.

"Sure."

They sat at the desk and had their coffee.

"I heard one of the Milligans call you Frank," Roper finally said. "Twice."

"I thought you might have."

"I've seen you before, but I couldn't place you until he called you Frank. What brought you here to wear a badge under the name 'Howard'?"

"When Jesse was killed, I was lost," Frank said. "I did my time and didn't know what to do with myself."

"I thought you were never convicted," Roper said. "Never did any time in a penitentiary."

"That's true," Frank said, "but I was in jail a year waitin' for my trial. Believe me, don't ever let anybody tell you that ain't servin' time."

"So what happened when you got out?"

"I lived with my ma for a while, then didn't know what to do with myself. I decided to come back to Missouri, but I came here to Festus, where nobody knew me."

"And took the name 'Howard'?"

Frank shrugged.

"My way of honoring Jesse's memory, I guess."

Jesse James had been living as "Thomas Howard" when he was shot in the back by Robert Ford.

"And the drinking?"

"I get depressed," Frank said, "but thanks to you, I think I can come out of it."

"What will you do now?"

"I guess the question is, what will you do?" Frank asked Roper.

"You mean, will I tell anyone that Frank James is the sheriff of Festus, Missouri?" Roper shook his head. "You helped me out, Frank. If you want to stay here as Tom Howard, that's up to you."

"Thanks. The only others who knew who I was were the Milligans."

"Terry?"

"No," Frank said, "Stu and Ned. We had worked with them once."

"And they never told anyone?"

"I guess not."

"Because of some sort of outlaw code?"

"Who knows?" Frank asked. "Maybe that was their way of honoring Jesse's memory."

"Well," Roper said, standing up. "I appreciate your help, Frank. Whatever you decide, I wish you luck."

The two men shook hands and Frank James—one half of the most famous set of outlaw brothers—said, "Thanks. I'll get your prisoners now."

1

When Roper entered his office on West Colfax, he was surprised to find it clean but empty. Apparently Mrs. Batchelder
had been letting her girls in to clean but, from the look of
the secretary's desk, not to do actual work. Of course, with
him gone for so long, there was not much in the way of work
to do except some filing, and message taking.

Mrs. Batchelder's school was only about a block or so
away, but he decided not to drop in there. It was midday and
he had literally just gotten back into town, so he went into
his office to have a look at his own desk.

He found half a dozen telegrams stacked there. The first
one shocked him, the subsequent ones surprised him. They
had all come in over the past two days. He took off his
jacket, hung it on the back of his chair, and sat down.

He was seated behind his desk, examining the messages
for a second time, when he heard the outer door to the office
open and close. He wondered if it was one of Mrs.

Batchelder's girls, but it was a man who appeared in his doorway to peer in tentatively.

"Hello?"

"Come on in," Roper said.

He stood up as the well-dressed man stepped into the office. His suit was expensive—more expensive than the three-piece suit Roper was wearing himself—and so was his haircut. He appeared to be in his early thirties, and ill at ease.

"Mr. Roper?"

"That's right," Roper said. "And you are?"

"Oh, yes, sorry," the man said. He came toward the desk and handed Roper a business card. It had the name "Eric Masters" on it, and the name of the law firm "Hastings, Pierce and Block." Roper knew they were a local firm with offices on Market Street. Since Masters's name was not on the masthead of the firm, Roper assumed he was an associate.

Half of the clients Roper entertained were lawyers, so the man's occupation did not surprise him.

"Have a seat, Mr. Masters, and tell me what brings you here."

The man sat down, still looking uncomfortable. Roper sat, unhappy that someone had walked into his office just moments after his arrival. It made him feel as if his office was being watched.

"My firm represents the Pinkerton Agency here in Denver," Masters said.

"Is that so?" Roper fingered the messages on his desk. He didn't believe in coincidence, so now he was sure his office had been under observation. It annoyed him that he hadn't seen it for himself when he arrived.

"Yes," Masters said, "I've been authorized to give you this." He took an envelope from his pocket and set it on the desk. It was thick, unsealed. Roper picked it up and looked inside. Most of the thickness came from cash.

"There is also a train ticket in there, to Chicago," Masters said.

Roper put the envelope back down.

"William and Robert would like you to attend their father's funeral," Masters said.

"Why?" Roper asked.

The first telegram he'd read had informed him that Allan Pinkerton had died. That was a shock. He knew Pinkerton, had worked for him both during the war and after. They had never gotten along, but he did learn from the man, and hearing that he had died at sixty-five years of age was a shock. The message was from William Pinkerton.

The other telegrams were from William and Robert, asking him to come to Chicago.

"I, uh, wasn't given a reason," he said. "I assume it's to show respect?"

"I can show respect by sending flowers," Roper said.

"Really?" Masters said, taken aback by the comment.

"Yes," Roper said. "Robert and William want me there for another reason."

"What would that be?"

"I don't know," Roper said.

"I am required to ask if you will be going," the lawyer said.

"If I am, I'll send a telegram to the Pinkertons," Roper said.

"But sir," the young lawyer said, "I'm supposed to—"

"You've done your job, Mr. Masters," Roper said. He put his hand on the envelope. "I'll keep this until I make up my mind. If I don't make the trip, I'll send this back to your offices by messenger."

"Er—" Masters said, confused.

"Just go, Mr. Masters," Roper said. "Go."

"Um, yes sir," Masters said. He stood, still looking confused. For a moment it seemed that he would speak again, but abruptly he turned and walked out. Roper waited for the outer door to open and close, then got up, walked into the outer office, and locked that door.

He went back to his desk, where he set the pile of telegrams next to the envelope containing the money and the rail ticket. He took the ticket out, saw that it was for the next morning.

Abruptly, he got to his feet, took his jacket from the back of his chair, and donned it. It hid the Colt he wore in a shoulder rig. He folded the telegrams, stuck them in the envelope with the money and the ticket, and put the whole thing in his inner pocket.

Still concerned that his office might have an observer, he used the secret door that led to the alley next to the building, and then to the street behind it.

When he came out onto the street, he looked both ways, across and up on the rooftops. Satisfied that no one was watching, he turned right and headed up the street.

2

Roper paused to look again, behind him, above him, saw no one, and entered the building that housed Mrs. Batchelder's School for Girls.

As he entered the office, a girl looked up at him and smiled. Mrs. Batchelder did not employ a receptionist. She used her own girls for that job. As usual, this one was pretty, even with her auburn hair pinned up over her head in what Roper thought was too old a style for her.

"Can I help you, sir?"

"Yes, I'd like to see Lily." He saw the confused look on the girl's face and beat her to the punch. "Mrs. Batchelder."

"Oh, yes, sir," she said. "Do you have an appointment?"

"I don't," he said, "but tell her Talbot Roper is here."

"Oh, Mr. Roper!" the girl said. She colored from her neck up. "Of course. Um, go right in."

The door to the left led to Lily Batchelder's office. The other doors led to different rooms she used for training her girls.

"Thank you."

He went to the door, knocked, and entered. Lily Batchelder looked up from her desk and smiled when she saw him. Not old enough to be Roper's mother, they had an older sister-younger brother type of relationship. It was an unlikely friendship that had served them both well over the past few years.

"Tal, you're back. I assume you found your telegrams."

"I did."

"Odd that they'd come in just days before you got back."

He approached her desk and sat across from her.

"Odder still that I'd have a visitor just minutes after I got back."

She put her chin in her hand and eyed him. A lock of hair fell across her forehead from the same hairdo as the girl outside, only it fit her better.

"You think your office is being watched?"

"I do," he said. "Have any of your girls commented on it?"

"There hasn't been much for the girls to do, except collect those telegrams, but none of them said anything to me. But they're not the most, uh, observant girls."

"I know," Roper said.

"Who came to see you?"

"A lawyer representing the Pinkertons," he said, taking out the envelope and putting it on the desk. "He left me this."

She picked it up and looked inside, took out the ticket.

"That's a nice retainer," she said. "Unless it's just traveling money, then it's even better. And a ticket for tomorrow? They're pretty confident."

"Looks that way."

"What are you going to do?"

"I'm not sure."

"Well," she said, putting the ticket back and sliding the envelope over to him, "how do you feel about the old man's death?"

"Well, it's too bad, of course."

"He was your mentor."

Roper hesitated, then said, "If you want to look at it that way."

"Well, just because you didn't get along . . . I mean, you worked for him for a long time."

"So you think I should go."

She sat back in her chair, which creaked beneath her bulk, and waved her hands. "I'm not saying that, at all. That's up to you."

Roper frowned.

"Did you come here hoping I'd tell you what to do, Tal?" she asked.

"No."

"I didn't think so."

He picked up the envelope and stuck it back in his pocket.

"I suppose I should go."

"Why do you think the sons want you there?"

"I don't know," he said, "but it can't be good."

"Why don't you telegraph them and ask them?" she suggested.

"No," he said, "I'll just telegraph them that I'm coming, I guess I should pay my respects to the old bulldog."

"Too bad," she said. "You just got back. Denver's missed you."

"And I've missed Denver," he said, "but I'll be right back after the funeral."

She gave him a look that clearly said, "You hope."

Roper left Mrs. Batchelder's building, once again alert for anyone watching him. Satisfied that he was safe from prying eyes he left and caught a cab to his own building, where he maintained rooms. He didn't go in, choosing first to go across the street to a small local café and have dinner.

Roper had three rooms, a living room, a bedroom, and a kitchen. He kept it clean and modestly furnished, his one splurge being a teak desk he kept in the living room, making it also his office at home. It was a new building, so he had indoor plumbing, and an elevator so he didn't have to walk up four flights. There was a back door, which he used to enter when he didn't want to be seen. He looked out his front window several times, but was finally satisfied that he wasn't being watched anymore. It had probably been only to determine when he got back to his office, so the lawyer, Masters, could visit him.

After that he made himself a pot of coffee and drank it while staring at the telegrams and the envelope containing the money and the ticket. Roper had served under Pinkerton—who had then gone by the name "Major E. J. Allen"—in the Union Army's new Secret Service. Afterward, he went back to running his Pinkerton Agency and recruited Roper to be one of his operatives. Roper worked under Pinkerton for several years, learning all that he could, and then quit to open his own agency. Although the two men never got along personally—Pinkerton thought Roper was too arrogant, Roper thought his boss was overbearing—they worked together well, and Pinkerton took his defection as a personal affront. They had seen each other infrequently over the intervening years leading up to Pinkerton's death.

Roper was curious as to how Pinkerton had met his end, but there was no information in any of the telegrams. In the end he decided to go if only to find out the whole story.

He packed a bag for the next day, and then turned in for the night.

The next morning, Roper caught the train to Saint Louis, and then changed for the train to Chicago, where he had been based while working for the Pinkerton Agency. His job had taken him all over the country and to other countries as well, but he'd only been back to Chicago once or twice, and not for a few years. Still, he knew his way around, and when he disembarked at Chicago's Union Station, he caught a cab and told the driver to take him to the Allerton Hotel on Michigan Avenue.

3

Before leaving Denver, Roper had sent a telegram to the Pinkertons telling them that he would be in Chicago for their father's funeral. He also told them, he'd be staying at the Allerton Hotel. When he checked in, the desk clerk handed him a message with his key.

He carried his own bag to his room, tossed it on the bed, and read the message. It was from William Pinkerton, telling Roper that the funeral would be at his father's home on West Adams Street the next afternoon.

Roper had a bath, changed his clothes, and went to see if his favorite steak house was still in business. It was on Rush Street, and he had a thick, sixteen-ounce steak. Most men he knew—especially Westerners—liked their steaks rare and bloody, but he liked his almost well done. It came smothered in onions and surrounded by potatoes and carrots, done to perfection.

Afterward he walked the city, to see what changes had occurred since he'd last been there. Chicago had become a hub for traveling, bringing people into the city in droves by both rail and ship. In addition, there were many new buildings needed to house the influx of industry, including the

new "Skyscraper," on LaSalle Street, the ten-story Home
Insurance Building, which was the first building ever to have
a structural steel frame. He was sure there would be many
more buildings like it erected as Chicago continued to grow
"upward," reaching for the sky. Roper was already unhappy
with the appearance of three-story buildings in Denver,
especially the ones where elevators were installed. He preferred to use the stairs in such buildings, but that might not
be an option in buildings of ten stories or more.

He walked down Rush Street, stopped in a small saloon
he used to frequent. There were no familiar faces there,
which suited him just fine. He had a beer and then walked
back to his hotel. He'd begun rereading Mark Twain's *Life
on the Mississippi* on the train and was halfway through it.
He read it until he got sleepy, then turned in.

Tomorrow promised to be a long day.

Roper arrived early at Pinkerton's palatial home on West
Adams. The old boy had done very well for himself. A man
in a suit nodded to him as he went through the front door.

"Have you seen William or Robert yet?" Roper asked.

"Yes, sir, they're inside."

"Thanks."

Roper went inside, where people were milling about, the
men dressed like himself in dark suits, the women in demure
but—in some cases—expensive dresses. Some of the men
were holding drinks, and Roper eventually tracked down
the source, a bar set up in one of the rooms.

He got himself a whiskey and listened to the talk in the
room. He heard several different versions of Allan Pinkerton's cause of death, including a stroke. He knew Allan
had suffered one in 1869, after which he had pretty much
turned over the operation of the agency to his sons, William
and Robert.

"Roper," he heard someone say.

He turned, drink in hand, and saw Allan Pinkerton's
older son approaching him. William was tall and slender, a

couple of years under forty, with dark hair that came to a widow's peak.

He put his hand out and Roper shook it.

"Thanks for coming," William said.

"It seemed fairly important to you and your brother," Roper said. "I got back from out of town and found your telegrams."

"We figured you must've been out on a case somewhere. I'm glad you were able to make it."

"Just barely," Roper said. "Got here yesterday."

A tall, gray-haired man appeared at William's elbow and said, "It's time, William."

"Roper, this is the Reverend Dr. Thomas. He's going to perform the service. Reverend, this is Talbot Roper, an old friend of the family."

"Sir."

"I'll be right there," William said to the reverend, who nodded and withdrew.

Roper was surprised by the sobriquet "old friend of the family" as it came out of William's mouth.

"Roper, Robert and I would like to talk to you. Would you have a late dinner with us tonight?"

"Sure," Roper said. "Why not?"

"Good."

"How did your dad die anyway?" he asked. "I've heard several different stories."

"Tonight," William said, putting his hand on Roper's arm. "You'll hear everything tonight."

William left the room, and a procession of people followed, including Roper.

In another room—this one with high ceilings—Allan Pinkerton lay in a casket at the front. William joined Robert and their sister, Cecily, and her family in a front row of seats. Allan Pinkerton's wife had preceded him to the grave earlier that year.

Roper deliberately sat in the back row during the service, which was dignified and short. The reverend did all the talking, with Allan's sons choosing to remain silent. The sound of Cecily's sobbing filled the room, her husband cradling her.

When it was over, Roper stood up quickly and made his way out before the crowd. He was sure there were statesmen and celebrities in attendance, but he didn't recognize any. He got himself outside the building before anyone else, and stood off to the side.

Pallbearers carried Pinkerton's casket to a horse-drawn hearse and loaded it on the back.

"He'll be taken to Graceland Cemetery."

Roper turned, saw Robert Pinkerton standing next to him. A couple of years younger than William, he was also tall and slender.

"You don't need to go there if you don't want to," Robert said.

"Thanks," Roper said. "I think I will pass."

"It's mostly family and close friends anyway."

Obviously, Robert did not think of Roper as a "close friend of the family."

"Will says you'll have dinner with us."

"That's right."

"Would you mind meeting us at eight? At the Firehouse?"

Roper had eaten once or twice at the Chicago Firehouse Steakhouse during his time in the city.

"I'll be there."

"Thank you."

Robert turned and hurried after his father's hearse.

Roper watched it drive away, after which the crowd dispersed and he was soon standing there alone.

Or so he thought.

4

The girl was small, dressed in a suit that was not as expensive as most had been. It was gray, very businesslike, with a skirt length that was more modest than modern. Hemlines were leaning toward daring these days, but this gal—while she had good legs—had not jumped on the bandwagon.

She was standing across from him, on the other side of the steps, holding her purse in front of her and staring at him.

At least, he thought she was staring at him. He looked around and there was no one else there, so she must have been staring at him.

He decided to find out the easy way, by asking.

He crossed in front of the concrete steps to her side, and she didn't move.

"Talbot Roper," he said, introducing himself.

"I know," she said. "I recognize you."

"From what?"

"I've seen your picture in the newspapers," she said.

"Then you have me at a disadvantage."

She had a stern look on her pretty face, and maintained it as she stuck her hand out and said, "I'm Dol."

"Doll?"

"Dol Bennett. Dorothea, that is, but everyone calls me Dol. Spelled D-o-l."

Roper shook her hand.

"Were you waiting here to talk to me?"

"I was, yes," she said, "but I admit, I didn't know how to approach you."

"Well," he said, "this'll do, I suppose. What's on your mind?"

"Lunch, I guess," she said. "I mean, I'll buy lunch. That just seems the easiest way to talk. I mean, rather than standing here on the street . . ."

He didn't know if she was normally this chatty, or if she was nervous, but he said, "Lunch is fine. Do you know a place?"

"I do, yes," she said. "It's just down the street. May I lead you there?"

"Yes," he said, "you may."

She nodded and started walking. Rather than actually allowing her to lead, he walked next to her.

The place turned out to be about four blocks away. It was very nondescript, no sign with the name above the door, just a doorway in a brick front. He would have walked right by it, never suspecting it was a café.

"How did you ever find this place?" he asked as they stopped.

"Allan used to take me here."

Allan? Before he could ask, she opened the door and entered without waiting for him to play the gentleman.

The inside was dark and cool. Each small table had a lamp with a green shade in the center, and off to one side a mahogany bar ran the length of the room. The bartender wore a white shirt, black vest, and black bow tie. He simply nodded at them as they took a table. There were about ten tables, and only two others were taken, one by a lone man, another by a couple.

"Did you say Allan Pinkerton showed you this place?" he asked.

"We used to come here to talk."

"We're talking about Allan Pinkerton, right?" Roper asked. "Brusque, impatient, unpleasant man?"

She smiled and said, "I'm sorry, but that was not the Allan I knew."

The bartender came over and asked, "What can I get you?"

"Brandy, please," Dol said.

"Beer," Roper said.

"Comin' up."

"Dol," Roper said, "I've got a lot of questions, starting with who you are and why you had a . . . relationship with Allan Pinkerton?"

"First," she said, "I'm a Pink."

"What?"

"An operative."

"For the Pinkertons?" he asked, aware that the question was inane.

She nodded. "Allan hired me."

"When?"

"Several months ago."

"Have you had many assignments since then?"

"No," she said. "William runs the Chicago office, and he doesn't like me. He couldn't fire me because of Allan, but he doesn't assign me to anything."

"And what's going on with you and Allan?" Roper asked. "That is, what *was* going on?"

"Oh," she said, staring at him, and then, "Oh! No, no, nothing like that!"

"I'm sorry," he said, "but—"

"No, no," she said, "Allan had been lonely since his wife died. We started to talk, that's all. Whenever he came to the offices, he'd stop by my desk and talk to me. One day he asked me if we could have lunch. I thought . . . well, like you—but that wasn't it, at all. He was a perfect gentleman. He just wanted to talk. Soon, it became a regular thing and he—knowing what people would think—started to bring me here, where no one would see us."

The bartender came over, set the drinks down, and withdrew. Roper didn't know if the man remembered Dol from other visits, but he acted like he'd never seen her before. The man was obviously good at his job.

"Well then," Roper said, "if you talked with him so much, maybe you can tell me how he died?"

"That's just it," she said. "I don't know. It's what I want to find out."

"And you thought I'd know?"

"If you don't," she said, "you will, as soon as they tell you. Then you can tell me."

"That's all you want?"

"Yes."

"You don't want me to talk to William about your work?"

"I'm quite sure the first thing William is going to do when he gets back to the office is fire me."

"And why would he do that?"

She hesitated, then said, "Let's just say he's not the gentleman his father was, and leave it at that."

William? Roper thought. The married, with children, William Pinkerton making advances toward one of his female operatives? That didn't sound like the man Roper knew, but then the Allan Pinkerton whom Dol knew was certainly not the same man whom Roper knew. The two of them had very different experiences with the Pinkertons.

"You are seeing them later, aren't you?" she asked.

"Yes," he said, "for dinner."

"I thought so."

"Do you know what they want with me?" he asked. "Why they were so anxious for me to come to their father's funeral?"

"Not specifically," she said. "I just know there's a job they don't feel they have the right man—or woman—for. I believe they're going to offer you the job."

"Well," he said, "they'll be pretty disappointed when I turn it down."

"But you have no idea what job they are going to offer you," Dol said.

"It doesn't matter," Roper said. "I'm not a Pinkerton operative."

"Why did you quit?" she asked. "Allan said you were the best op he ever had."

"Did he?"

"I probably shouldn't have told you that," she said, "but since I did, I'll tell you this, too . . . it really hurt him when you left. He thought he'd be turning the agency over to you one day."

"I had to live my own life, Dol," Roper said. He didn't believe for a minute that Pinkerton would have handed the reins of the agency over to him and not his sons. If that's what he told Dol, then at least Roper now knew that Pinkerton had been telling her some giant fibs.

"Well," she said, "I suppose you did the right thing. They *do* consider you to be the best private detective in the country."

"So they say." He'd heard that, too, but he didn't know who "they" were.

"Listen," she said, "can we meet for breakfast tomorrow so you can tell me what they wanted you for?"

"If I say yes," he answered, "do I get more food for breakfast than I got for lunch today?"

She stared at him for a moment, then looked at the table and seemed to just realize that they had never ordered food.

"Oh my," she said, "I did invite you to lunch, didn't I?"

"Yes, you did."

"They have wonderful sandwiches here," she said. "Please, let me buy you lunch."

"Only because I'm hungry," he said, "and I'm starting to think I might not have much of an appetite tonight at dinner."

She smiled happily—which made her look impossibly young and pretty—and waved at the bartender.

5

After lunch Roper promised to meet Dol at his hotel for breakfast in the morning. He wasn't sure how much he would tell her. He wouldn't know that until after he talked with the Pinkerton brothers.

He offered to get a cab and drop her somewhere, but she refused and said she'd see him the next day. She hurried off after that, her heels echoing on the pavement.

Roper walked to the corner, flagged down a passing cab, and went back to his hotel.

He killed time finishing his Mark Twain, then washed and dressed for dinner. He went downstairs, had the doorman get him a cab to the Chicago Firehouse Steakhouse on South Michigan Avenue, even though he could have walked it.

As he entered, he looked around and spotted the brothers sitting toward the back. The Firehouse had a tuxedoed maître d', but he told the man, "I see my party."

"Who would that be, sir?" the man asked, not letting him pass.

Roper stopped, looked at the man, then decided to just let him do his job.

"The Pinkertons."

"Of course, sir," the man said. "This way."

He followed the man across the crowded room to the table, where both William and Robert looked up.

"Gentlemen, your guest has arrived."

"Thank you, Henry. Would you have the waiter bring us three brandies, please?" William asked.

"I'll have a beer, Henry," Roper said.

"Of course," William said. "Two brandies and a beer, Henry."

"Yes, sir."

He gave Roper—his suit and his choice of beverage—a condescending look and walked away.

"Have a seat, Talbot," William said.

The brothers were seated opposite each other. Roper sat down next to Robert, with William across from him.

"Again," William said, "thank you for coming—to Chicago, to the funeral, and to dinner."

"I have to admit my curiosity is up."

"Curious about what, in particular?" Robert asked.

"Well, what was so all fired important that I come to Chicago, how Allan died and . . . well, that's it, for a start."

William chose to answer the last question first.

"We're still not sure what we're going to tell the public," he said. "The fact is Allan had a fall three weeks ago, and bit his tongue. I mean, he bit through his tongue."

"How bad a fall?"

"Not that bad, really," William said, "but his tongue became infected and . . . well, it became gangrenous and he . . . died."

Roper stared at the two of them.

"Wait a minute," he said. "You're telling me he died because . . . he bit his tongue?"

William and Robert exchanged a look.

"I heard at the wake that he had a stroke."

"Not true," Robert said, "but we may go with that story."

"Maybe he had a stroke, which caused his fall, which caused him to . . ."

William was shaking his head.

"I also heard at the wake something about foul play."

"The doctor assured us it was the tongue," William said.

"That's . . . that's . . . tragic," Roper said.

"Exactly," Robert said.

The waiter came with their drinks, and William looked at Roper and said, "Do you mind if I order for all of us?"

"No, go ahead."

"Three steak dinners, Andy."

"Yes, sir."

Roper sipped his beer, still stunned by the news of what had caused Pinkerton's death. Maybe he and Allan hadn't gotten along, but what a waste for a man to die in his sixties in that way.

"As for your other question," William said "we have a proposition for you."

It looked as if Dol was right. They were going to offer him a job. He contrived to look more interested in his beer than in what they had to say.

The brothers exchanged a glance, and Robert nodded. Roper took this to mean that William would be taking the lead. They were, after all, in his backyard. Robert ran the San Francisco office. Roper had been expecting for a long time that the Pinkertons would open a Denver office. He wondered if they would ever ask him to run it, now that Allan was dead. Allan, himself, would have opened it just to compete with him.

"I'm listening."

"We have clients in Fort Worth who are being besieged by . . . well, let's say saboteurs."

"That's a fancy word," Roper said.

"The Union Stockyard Company has plans to build a stockyard there," William said. "Mike Hurley is the president of the company. He's looking for investors— big-time investors—to back the construction. To that end, he's going to be playing host to possible investors, including a Boston bigwig named Greenleaf Simpson. Now Simpson, should he invest, has plans to stop shipping the cattle out of Fort Worth and start butchering and packaging it locally."

"So Fort Worth would no longer just be a stopping-off point," Roper said.

"Correct," William said. "This could mean big money for Fort Worth, and for Texas."

"And somebody's trying to ruin that?"

"Definitely."

"What kind of sabotage are we talking about?"

"Dead and mutilated cattle, fires, murder—"

"Murder is more than sabotage," Roper said. "Who's investigating the murders?"

"The local police."

"Why not the federal marshals or Texas Rangers?"

"They haven't been called in."

"Yet," Robert said.

"But you assume they will?"

"Possibly," William said, "but even then, marshals are not detectives. Neither are Rangers."

"I suppose not."

"We've been engaged to root out the saboteurs," William said. "In doing that, we would put a stop to the fires, the dead cattle, and murder."

"So send someone."

"We don't have anyone to send," Robert said.

"You have two thousand men working for you," Roper said.

"Strike breakers," William said, "and manhunters. Not detectives."

"You've got to have somebody—"

"No one with your credentials," Robert said.

"But I'm not a Pinkerton," Roper pointed out.

"And you don't have to be," William said. "We're not asking you to join the agency. We're just proposing that we . . . subcontract you."

"I see."

"We can work out a satisfactory fee schedule," Robert said.

"Fee schedule," Roper repeated.

At that moment the waiter appeared with their dinners. The conversation—or perhaps "negotiation" would have been a better word—was suspended until he had finished and withdrawn.

6

"We know that your fees are high," Robert said after a few moments.

"Higher than yours?" Roper asked.

"That's not germane," Robert said. "We're willing to pay your fee."

"I don't know, fellas," Roper said, cutting into his steak. It was medium rare, but he didn't mind. After all, nobody asked him.

"Are you well known in Fort Worth?" William asked.

"I'm not, actually," Roper said. "In fact, I'm really not well known on sight anywhere."

"We understand that you are clever with disguises," Robert said.

"I've had my moments."

"Look," William said, "you can decide on your own approach to the job. Go in as yourself, or go in undercover. It's up to you."

Roper chewed his steak and regarded the two brothers.

"There's something else going on here," he said.

"What do you mean?" Robert asked.

"Don't you find this unusual?" Roper asked. "That the

Pinkertons would try to subcontract me? Me, of all detectives in the country? Why not Heck Thomas? Frank Dodge? Jim Hume?"

William hesitated, then said, "You're better." Roper could see how much it hurt the man to say it. It almost broke his jaw. And Robert was grinding his teeth.

"What do you say, Roper?" William asked.

"I say I'll have to think about it."

"How long?"

"Just overnight," Roper said. "I'm not looking to stay in Chicago much beyond that."

William and Robert exchanged another of their glances.

"All right," William said. "Can we meet tomorrow?"

"I'll come to your offices," Roper said, cutting into his steak again. "This steak is excellent."

"Yes," Robert agreed, "the steaks are very good here."

"Very well," William said, "we'll see you at the office tomorrow . . . morning?"

"Sure, why not?" Roper asked. "Let's say in the morning."

"Very good," William said.

"After breakfast."

"Yes."

They fell into an awkward silence as they began to eat in earnest. Roper decided to keep them talking to him, even if they really didn't want to.

"So how do you boys figure to divvy up the agency?" he asked.

They both looked up from their plates and William said, "Oh, probably as we have it. I will stay here in Chicago, and Robert will handle the San Francisco office."

"Any thoughts of expansion?" Roper asked. "New York? Denver?"

"To expand," Robert said, "we would have to have someone we trusted to run those offices."

"And you don't?"

"Not yet," William said.

Roper studied the brothers while they ate. They answered

whatever question he posed, but did not instigate any conversation of their own. Roper knew that Allan had had a high opinion of his abilities. He probably had not, as Dol had proposed, any intention of turning the agency over to him, but he was sure the boys had heard enough about him from the old man to resent him. It must have been killing them to ask him for his help.

He pondered the question while they ate. He wondered if their big money clients had perhaps mentioned the possibility of hiring him instead of them. Maybe this was a last-ditch effort to actually get the job? By promising that he would be involved. Or maybe Talbot Roper was starting to have an exaggerated opinion of his own worth. Of course, it would be nice if that was the case.

"What about women?" he asked suddenly.

"What?" Robert asked.

"I'm sorry?" William asked.

"Female operatives," Roper said. "How many do you have?"

"Uh, a few," William said.

"None in my office," Robert said. "It's no place for a woman."

"Hmm," Roper said, "maybe William doesn't agree. Or was it Allan who hired the women that you do have?"

"I, uh, have an open mind," William said. "There might be some assignments that would be more suited to a woman's talents."

"Hmph," Robert said.

Roper wondered if this question had been a bone of contention between the boys and their father? Maybe Dol would have the answer to that.

Roper decided to leave the boys alone and enjoy his own dinner.

After dinner the three of them left the restaurant and stopped outside for the doorman to hail them a cab. William and Robert were sharing one.

"How is your family taking it?" Roper asked.

"Cecily is not doing well," William said.

"We are handling it," Robert assured Roper. "Our father would not want us to let the business suffer."

"I'm sure," Roper said.

"Where are you staying?" William asked.

"The Allerton."

"Second rate," Robert opined. "I prefer the Drake."

"I like the Allerton," Roper said.

Robert shrugged and said, "To each his own."

He watched the two brothers load into a cab, and then William turned and said to him, "See you in the morning."

Roper nodded and the cab drove away.

"Cab, sir?" the doorman asked.

It was July in Chicago but it felt more like spring.

"No thanks," he said, "I think I'll walk."

7

Roper tried to read that night—another Twain, this one *Punch, Brothers, Punch! and Other Sketches*, a short story collection—but he couldn't keep his mind on it. There was something else going on with the Pinkerton brothers. He was sure of that, or they wouldn't be asking for his help. Before he agreed to do this for them, he was going to have to get that out in the open.

He took the book to bed with him, but didn't last long. He set it aside, doused the light, and went to sleep.

When he came down to the lobby at eight, Dol Bennett was waiting.

"We didn't set a time," he said. "Did we?"

"No," she said, "but you strike me as an early riser."

"You mind having breakfast here?"

"No," she said, "you're buying this time, right?"

He smiled. "Right."

They went into the dining room. She was wearing another suit like the one she'd been wearing yesterday, this one brown. Before sitting, though, she removed the jacket, revealing a light blue blouse underneath. It looked like silk to Roper. He was wearing his best three-piece blue suit for his visit to the Pinkerton offices. He had a cut-down Colt in a shoulder rig underneath.

"They must be paying Pinkertons well, these days," he said.

She knew what he meant, and said, "I have my own money. An inheritance."

"Good for you."

"There's no law against dressing well."

"No, there isn't."

When the waiter came, she ordered a poached egg and some toast. Roper asked for chicken-fried steak and eggs, but was told they didn't have it. He'd forgotten where he was. "Make it steak and eggs," he said. He almost asked for grits, but that would have been another mistake.

"Yes, sir," the waiter said. "Coffee?"

They both said yes.

"So," she said, "how was dinner last night?"

"My steak was underdone," he said, "but it was edible."

"What about the company?"

"Stiff," Roper said, "and uncomfortable."

"But you got through."

"I finished my dinner."

"Did they make an offer?"

"They sure did."

"I knew it!"

"Do you know what case?"

She hesitated, then said, "I have an idea."

Roper didn't comment.

"Fort Worth?"

"You got it," he said.

The waiter came with their coffee. They leaned back in their seats to let him pour.

"What did you say?" she asked when the waiter was gone.

"I told them I'd give them my answer today."

"I could do that job," she said.

"Could you?"

"I know I could."

"In the stockyards of Forth Worth?" he asked. "How would you fit in?"

"Undercover," she said. "I could go in as a . . . a clerk, or something. Maybe a saloon girl."

"You'd never pass as a saloon girl."

"Roper," she said, "you have to take this assignment."

"I do?"

"Yes," she said, "and tell them you want to take me with you."

"Is that what this was all about?" he asked. "Lunch? Breakfast? Did you really have a relationship with Allan?"

"That's true," she said. "We talked, and that was all. But even he wouldn't speak up for me when it came to assignments. He just made sure they kept me on the payroll."

"So you need this assignment to keep your job."

She hesitated, then said, "Yes."

"Dol," he said, "even if I take the assignment, I wouldn't take you with me."

"But . . . why?"

"Because I could get myself killed while I'm looking out for you."

"You wouldn't have to look out for me," she assured him. "I can take care of myself."

"That may be—" he said, but stopped as the waiter came with their food.

Once the waiter was gone, he said, "Eat your breakfast."

"But—"

He cut into his steak.

They remained silent until the waiter removed their plates and poured more coffee for them.

"So what are you going to do?" she asked.

"I'm not sure."

"You haven't made up your mind?"

"No."

"Why wouldn't you just say no?"

"There's something else going on," he said. "Something else behind their offer. I want to find out what that is."

"So what are you doing today?"

"I'm going up to the offices to see William and Robert."

"You think they'll tell you what you want to know?"

"If they want me badly enough," he said, "yes."

He paid the bill and they walked outside.

"When are you going?" she asked.

"Right from here."

"We can share a cab."

"You don't mind being seen with me?"

"We don't have to go into the building together," she said.

8

The cab drew to a stop in front of headquarters of the Pinkerton Detective Agency, on Washington and Dearborn in downtown Chicago. Roper stepped down, helped Dol down, then turned and looked up at the big Eye logo on the three-story facade, accompanied by the words "We Never Sleep."

"Nobody ever said Allan was subtle," he said.

"What?" Dol asked.

"Never mind."

"I'm going across the street for coffee," she said. "I'll come inside in a few minutes."

"Fine," he said, "I'll be in William's office, I guess."

"Perhaps I'll see you inside," she said, and walked across the street.

Roper turned and went inside. He found the reception area in front of William's third-floor office and presented himself to the woman there, a thickset, middle-aged lady with big horn-rimmed glasses.

"I'm here to see Mr. William Pinkerton," he said.

"And your name?"

"Talbot Roper."

"Oh," she said, "yes. One moment."

Her pause spoke volumes. He waited while she entered the office behind her, and then reappeared in moments, looking chagrined. Perhaps she'd been chastised for keeping him waiting.

"Please go in, Mr. Roper," she said, with a lot more respect than she had originally shown him.

"Thank you."

When he entered, he found both William and Robert waiting for him. William was seated behind a large, oak desk, while Robert was standing in front of the plate glass window. Roper wondered if he had seen him and Dol arrive together.

"Good morning, gentlemen," Roper said.

"Morning," William said.

Robert just turned and nodded, keeping his arms folded tightly. Roper had the feeling the brothers had been having a contentious moment before he arrived. Maybe one of them wanted him to take the assignment, and one of them didn't. His vote went to Robert for the dissenting vote.

"Well," William said, "I expect you've made your decision."

"Not yet."

"Why not?" Robert demanded.

"You mind if I sit?"

"Of course not," William said, "Sit Can we get you anything?"

"No," Roper said, sitting across from the older Pinkerton brother, "I just had breakfast."

William nodded.

"I need more information before I make my decision," Roper said.

The brothers had one of those moments of exchanging a glance.

"What kind of information?" William asked.

"Whatever it is you're not telling me," Roper said. "We all know you two would never ask me for anything without a damn good reason."

Robert turned to look out the window again. William drummed his fingers on the desk.

"There's pressure," Roper said. "I want to know from whom."

"We have to tell him," William said to his brother.

Robert shrugged without turning.

"You're right," William said. "Our client said they wanted the best."

"And they mentioned me?"

"You and Frank Geyer."

Roper knew Geyer. He was another former Pinkerton who had opened his own agency, this one in Philadelphia.

"Then why didn't they approach me or Geyer?" Roper asked.

William hesitated, then said, "It seems they want our organization behind your abilities as a detective."

"Mine or Frank's?"

"Either one."

"So the decision to approach me instead of Frank was whose?"

William hesitated.

"Oh, I get it," Roper said. "You went to Frank first and he turned you down."

Neither man replied.

"Come on, boys."

"Frank doesn't like Robert," William said.

"And the feeling is mutual."

"But you guys don't like me either," Roper said, "and I'm really not crazy about either of you."

"Our father had more respect for you than he did Frank Geyer," William said.

"Then why did you go to Frank first?"

"He was closer," Robert said. "There was a chance you wouldn't make it here in time."

"In time for the funeral?"

"Or the job," William said. "Our clients are getting . . . impatient."

Roper knew he could have demanded to know who

the clients were. All the clients, since there was obviously more than one. But that didn't matter much to him. If he took the job, he'd be dealing with the Pinkertons.

And he was considering taking the job, although he wasn't sure why. Maybe that was something he'd have to discover about himself later. He hadn't been to Fort Worth in a while, not since it had become more than just a stopover for the cattle on its way to the Kansas City railhead.

"What do you say, Roper?" William asked.

Robert turned to receive his answer. He was still grinding his teeth.

"Why don't we sit down," Roper said, "and hash out that fee schedule you mentioned."

9

Fort Worth, Texas

Talbot Roper was in his early forties, tall, handsome, clean shaven, and usually well dressed. "Andy Blake" was in his mid-forties, tall, rumpled looking with hair slightly graying and receding, grayish beard stubble, and dressed in threadbare clothes that might have been expensive once, but had seen better days.

After establishing his "fee schedule" with the Pinkertons, Roper had gone back to his hotel room to figure out his approach. The Pinkertons got him railroad tickets to get him as close to Fort Worth as they could, after which he would ride in. In the end, Roper had decided to ride into Forth Worth as "Andy Blake," leaving Talbot Roper, his clothes, his guns, and his horse behind. He rode an old sorrel, carried a worn Colt on his hip, wore sweat-stained clothes and hat. He figured to get a job in the stockyards, start his investigation there.

But first he had to establish his new identity, get a hotel room, and start drinking as Andy Blake.

* * *

Fort Worth was an experience for the olfactory senses. The aroma from the stockyards—largely manure—permeated almost the entire city. And it certainly added to the dubious attractions of the area known as "Hell's Half Acre."

The Half Acre was located between the railroad station and Courthouse Square, and was the place the cowboys, drovers, railroad workers, firefighters, stockyard workers, and gamblers went to sow their wild oats. There were plenty of saloons, gambling halls, and bordellos to accommodate them all.

The place he chose to do his drinking was a saloon called the Bullshead. Roper was only standing at the bar for a few moments, still nursing his first beer, when he realized he was in the right place. Behind him was an entire table of men who worked in the stockyards. If the smell wasn't a dead giveaway, their conversation—loud and bawdy—certainly did.

As "Andy Blake," Roper decided to drink for a couple of days before making any contact with the stockyard workers. After that he'd try to get a job there himself, but first he needed to make some friends.

On the third day in town, he made his move . . .

He waited until the Bullshead was in full swing, the noise deafening, the smoke suffocating, the gambling intense. Saloon girls were sashaying around the room, delivering drinks and avoiding the grasp of most of the customers.

One girl—a willowy blonde with a pretty face—came over and leaned on the bar next to him.

"This is your third night here," she said.

"Is it?"

"I seen you the last two nights," she said. "What's your game?"

"What do you mean?"

"You just stand here and drink," she said. "You don't gamble, you don't grab at the girls."

"I'm new in town," he said. "I'm just tryin' to get my bearings."

She studied him, looking him up and down, and said, "You don't feel right."

Just what he needed, a saloon girl with good instincts.

"Would you like it better if I grabbed you?" he asked with a leer.

"I might," she said, "but I don't think you would. You look like a man with class who's slummin'."

"Don't you have some work to do?" he asked. "Somebody's lap to sit in?"

She grinned and said, "Yeah, I do, but I ain't done with you." She closed one eye. "My name's Nancy. I'll figure out your game. You wait and see."

He watched her walk away and changed his plans for the night.

From observing the men for three days, he had made his choice. There was a big, loud fella who sat with the stockyard crew who always looked ready for a fight. He drank a lot, grabbed at the girls, and wasn't very smart. He figured picking a fight with this guy would make an impression on the stockyard crew. But now that Nancy was keeping an eye on him, he figured he better put it off for another night.

He finished his beer, paid his bill, and left the saloon, deciding to call it a night.

He'd gotten himself a room in a dive near the stockyards, close enough to be able to smell the manure. As he walked from the saloon to his hotel, he became aware that somebody was following him.

He wasn't happy with the thought that somebody might have picked him out already. It was bad enough that the saloon girl, Nancy, had a feeling about him. But what else could it be? He certainly did not look like somebody who would be worth robbing.

He had already checked out the area around his hotel, the saloon, and in Hell's Half Acre in general, so he knew there were some streets that would be pretty well deserted this time of the evening. He turned down one of those streets, mindful of the sound of footsteps behind him.

Fort Worth had not yet gone to concrete sidewalks, so the footsteps echoed nicely on the boardwalk. From the sound, Roper deduced that the person following him was slight, with short strides.

Eventually, he rounded a corner and came to an alley he could step into. The footsteps came closer and closer, rushing just a bit as the person came to the corner. As they came around, Roper stepped out, sneaked his arm around the person's neck. As he'd suspected, they were short and slight and didn't offer much in the way of resistance beyond some feeble struggling. Roper dragged them farther into the alley.

"Just relax," Roper said, "and tell me why you're following me."

The person gurgled a bit, as Roper's forearm was pressing against their windpipe. Abruptly, their hat fell off and Roper found his nose in a tangle of fragrant hair. It was then he also noticed some lumps that would be odd for a man to have.

He released the person and turned them around. The alley was dark, but he was fairly certain he was looking into the red and mottled face of Dol Bennett.

"What the hell—" he said.

"You almost choked me to death," she complained.

"Dol," he said, "I could've killed you."

"It feels like you tried!"

"What the hell are you doing here?"

"Can we go someplace and talk?" she asked. "And where I can get some water?"

"Damn it—" he said. "All right. This alley leads to the

back of my hotel. We'll go to my room so nobody sees us together."

"As long as you act like a perfect gentleman," she said.

"What the—"

"That means no choking."

He glared at her, then said, "I don't think I can promise that."

10

Once they were in his room with the lamp turned high, Roper could see that Dol was dressed much as he was so that, when she was wearing her hat, she looked like a short, disheveled man. With the hat off, he could see her feminine features clearly beneath the soot that covered her face.

The room had the bare minimum, a bed that was too small for Roper with a thin mattress, a flimsy chest with one drawer broken and hanging out, threadbare curtains on the single window, which had so much dirt on the glass it was almost opaque. The walls were so thin he could hear his neighbors with the whores they brought home at night. When he returned to the room and lit the lamp, insects skittered away back into the walls.

"Now," he said, "what the hell do you think you're doing?"

"Can I have some water?" she asked.

He poured her a glass and handed it to her. She drank half of it down and rubbed her neck tenderly.

"You've some grip," she said.

"I'm not going to apologize for that," he said. "I had no

idea who was following me, or why. You sounded like a herd of buffalo."

"I was just trying to catch up to you so we could talk," she said. "If I'd really wanted to follow you, you never would have known I was there."

He doubted that but decided to let it go.

"Just tell me what you want, Dol," Roper said, "and why you're trying to get yourself killed by walking around Hell's Half Acre dressed like that?"

"What do you mean?" she asked. "This is a great disguise."

He studied her critically. Despite the disheveled appearance, she still seemed feminine to him. Maybe that was just because he knew who she was. But she still seemed the type—small, helpless—who would become a victim in the Half Acre.

"Never mind," he said. "What do you want?"

"I want to work with you on this assignment."

"I don't have anything for you to do," he told her. "Does your boss know you're here?"

She frowned.

"William fired me as soon as you left."

"No connection to me, I gather?"

"No," she said, "he just said there was no place for me in the Pinkertons."

"So you want to prove him wrong."

"Yes! And I want you to help me."

"I can't do that, Dol," he said. "I have too much to do, not to mention keeping myself alive."

"I can watch your back!"

"I don't know that," Roper said, "and I can't depend on it. I think what you have to do is go home."

"Home?" she asked. "Where's that? I've got nothing left in Chicago."

"Where are you from?"

She frowned, almost pouted, and folded her arms.

"There's nothing for me there either."

"Do you have a place to stay?"

"I have a hotel room."

"Where?"

"The White Elephant."

"Why would you stay there," he asked, "when you're trying to blend in here in Hell's Half Acre? Why do you think I'm staying here?"

"I—I didn't think—"

"And it's that kind of not thinking that could get you killed. And me!"

"I'm sorry . . ."

"Go home, Dol," he said. "Go back east anyway. You're not going to do me or yourself any good here."

She just stood there, miserable.

"Do you have money?"

"Yes."

"Go back to your hotel, get yourself cleaned up, and have a meal. You'll feel better. Then go to the train station in the morning."

She nodded, turned toward the door.

"And go out the back, the way we came in," he said.

She nodded again and left without a word.

Outside the hotel, two men stared up at the single lit window.

"According to the clerk, that's his room," Ed Hague said.

"Okay," Dan Giles said, "we'll wait for it to go out before we go after him."

"You sure Nancy's right?" Hague asked. "This don't look like a place a fella with money would stay."

"She's a good judge of men," Giles said. "She says the guy ain't what he seems to be, that's good enough for me. She ain't steered me wrong yet."

"What's your deal with her?" Hague asked.

"She gets twenty percent," Giles said.

"That seems like a lot."

"This is your first job with me," Giles said. "You'll see that she earns her keep."

"I hope so," Hague said. "I need to have somethin' that's gonna pay."

"Don't worry," Giles said. "This pays."

They settled into their darkened doorway and waited for the light in the window to go out.

Dol went out the back door of the hotel, then used an alley along the side to get to the front. She was about to step out onto the boardwalk when she thought she saw something move across the street, in the shadows. She stepped back and waited, and sure enough, saw two men standing in a doorway, looking up at the hotel.

She had a feeling she knew what they were looking at, so she decided to settle in herself and see what was going to happen.

11

After Dol left, Roper sat down on the bed, which was so hard it barely sagged beneath his weight. The girl was lucky she had not already gotten herself killed. He hoped she would listen to his advice and leave Fort Worth.

He rubbed his hand over his face—actually "Andy Blake's" face—feeling the unfamiliar rasp of stubble on his palm. Tomorrow he'd have to go ahead and make his contact with the stockyard workers, but maybe he needed to do it at a different saloon, one where a saloon girl had not shown such interest in him. But he'd already put three days of research into this saloon and this group of men; he hated to waste the time.

He got undressed, doused the lamp, and got into bed. He hadn't brought anything to read, because it wouldn't do for "Andy Blake" to have Mark Twain or Charles Dickens in his room, just in case somebody came up to take a look.

He put his gun on the flimsy night table next to the bed and tried to go to sleep.

"There," Giles said, "the light went out."

"Let's go," Hague said, stepping from the doorway.

Giles grabbed his arm and pulled him back.

"We have to give him time to fall asleep," he said.

"If he's awake, we can just kill him," Hague said.

"I wanna do this without killin' him if we can," Giles said. "We're just tryin' to rob him."

"Killin' him would be a lot easier."

"And it would get the law on our asses," Giles said. "So far all I've done is rob people, and the law just figures that's the price of doin' business in the Half Acre. But if we kill him, that'll change."

Hague didn't appear to like the idea, but he said, "You're the boss."

Giles *was* the boss. The robberies were his idea, and he was starting to think that maybe Ed Hague wasn't the best recruit. After this one maybe he'd cut the man loose and look for someone else. Someone not quite so bloodthirsty.

"Fifteen minutes," he said to Hague, "we'll give it fifteen minutes."

Dol watched the two men, saw one step from the doorway and the other pull him back. They were planning something, something in that hotel. It may have had nothing to do with Roper, but she decided to stick around and make sure. If they *were* after Roper, maybe this was her chance to prove herself to him.

She touched the .32 Colt she had tucked into her belt. And hoped when the time came, it would be enough gun.

Giles nudged Hague, who actually seemed to have fallen asleep standing up.

"Let's move," he said.

"Finally."

They crossed the street and entered the hotel. The lobby was empty except for the clerk nodding off behind the cheap, flimsy front desk. There was a threadbare sofa with a cheap table in front of it, but that was it for lobby furniture. The hotel was mostly used by the higher-class whores who didn't work the streets.

The clerk looked up as they approached.

"Room six," he said.

"Thanks."

As they went up the stairs, Hague asked, "How much does he get?"

"Five percent."

"Yer givin' away a lot of your money."

"Yeah," Giles agreed, "I think maybe I am."

Dol watched the two men enter the hotel by the front door, then retraced her steps down the alley to the back door and let herself back in. She used the back stairs to get up to the second floor in time to see the men creeping along the hallway. When they stopped in front of a door, she felt sure it was Roper's.

She took the gun from her belt and started her own way down the hall.

Giles and Hague drew their guns, and Giles silently indicated to Hague that he should kick the door in. Hague nodded, backed up so that he was flat against the wall, then launched himself at the door. His feet struck it just below the doorknob and the door slammed open.

There was a flash of light from inside, and a bullet struck Hague dead center in his torso.

Giles panicked and turned to run, but Dol fired twice, hitting him both times and putting him down.

Roper was a notoriously light sleeper when he was working, and the fleabag hotel had noisy, creaky floorboards. He was aware as soon as the two men began creeping down the hall.

When the door slammed open, he fired one shot. He heard the other shots from the hall, and rushed out to see what was happening.

Dol ran down the hall, just as Roper came out his door. For a moment they pointed their guns at each other, then backed off.

"Don't worry," she said. "I got the other one."

"Damn it, Dol!" he said.

"What?" she asked, wide-eyed. "I helped you out here. I saw them outside and followed them in."

"I wanted one of them alive," he said. "I needed to find out if they were after me, or 'Andy.'"

"Who's Andy?" she asked.

Roper stared at her and said wearily, "Oh, Dol . . ."

12

Roper didn't have time to properly chastise Dol for what she had done. The truth of the matter was he would have been fine without her help.

"Get out," he told her, "before the law shows up."

"But—"

"I don't want to have to explain who you are," he said, "because I'm not going to explain who I am."

"Oh, all right," she said, "but—"

"We'll talk later," he promised her.

"Okay," she said happily, but he added, "Right before you get on the train to leave."

"But—"

"Go!" he snapped. "And use the back door."

A few of the other doors had opened and nervous-looking men had looked out, but Roper said, "Don't worry. It's got nothing to do with you."

So once Dol left, the hall was empty but for Roper and the two bodies. That made him suspicious. Why hadn't the desk clerk come running to see what happened? Maybe because he thought he already knew?

Before long a man with a badge came up the stairs and

stalked down the hall. By this time Roper had no gun in his hand and had adopted his "Andy Blake" persona.

"What the hell happened here?" the lawman asked. He was tall, slender, with the ferret face of someone who never looked happy. In his fifties, the sheriff, Roper assumed, had been wearing a badge for a long time. That could take all the joy out of a man for sure.

"I don't know, Sheriff," he said. "These fellas kicked in my door, and I defended myself." He hoped the man wouldn't be good enough to be able to tell that one of them had been shot from the hallway.

The lawman walked to each man, turned him over with his foot, and took a look.

"Do you know them?" Roper asked.

"I don't know this one," he said, "but this one's a two-bit bushwhacker, usually has different partners." He looked at Roper. "He usually targets people he knows have money. Were you flashin' a roll tonight at one of the saloons?"

"Not me," Roper said. "I ain't got a roll to flash. In fact, I'm lookin' for a job."

"What's your name?"

"Andy Blake."

"What are you doin' in town?"

"Like I said," Roper responded, "I'm lookin' for a job."

"Doin' what?"

"Whatever involves cattle," Roper said. "I done it all."

"So you're lookin' for a job in the stockyards?"

"I thought I'd start there."

"And you didn't come into contact with these jaspers tonight?"

"I never seen either one of them."

"Yeah, okay," the lawman said.

"What's your name?" Roper asked.

"Reynolds," the sheriff said. "You better talk to the clerk about gettin' another room. I'll have some men come up and move these bodies." Reynolds looked up and down the hall. Roper figured he was thinking about the fact that nobody was sticking their head out to see what was going on.

"Nobody showed much interest in the goings on, Sheriff."

"Naw, they wouldn't," Reynolds said. "The fellas in these rooms usually got somethin' on their minds." He looked at Roper. "You got a girl in your room?"

"No, sir," Roper said. "I was sleepin'."

"Yeah, okay," Reynolds said. "These two ain't gonna be no loss to anybody. Go get yerself another room key."

Roper went down to the lobby, which was still empty. Hearing shots in Hell's Half Acre was nothing new, but he still thought the clerk should have showed some interest.

The young man watched as Roper approached the front desk, his prominent Adam's apple bobbing.

"Guess you didn't hear the shots upstairs," Roper said.

"I heard 'em."

"Yeah? How come you didn't come runnin'?"

"This is the Half Acre, mister," the clerk said. "You don't run towards shots, you run away from 'em."

"Well, looks like I'll need another key," Roper said. "Those two broke my door."

"We got rooms," the clerk said. He turned, grabbed a key, and turned back, handing it to Roper. "There ya go."

"I guess when you gave those two my room number, you should've given them my key. Then they wouldn't have had to kick in my door."

"Huh?"

"They knew what room I was in because you told 'em," Roper said. "Now, when the sheriff comes down here I can tell him that, or I could keep quiet."

"Why would ya do that?"

"Because you're gonna tell me who you and those two are workin' with," Roper said. "Who sent them after me?"

"I can't—I'll get killed."

"Okay, then," Roper said, "I'll tell you, and you just nod." The young man didn't move.

"Go ahead, try it. Nod."

He nodded.

"Okay," Roper said, "it's my guess a young lady named Nancy sent those two after me after she saw me in the saloon."

The clerk remained frozen. There were footsteps on the stairs.

"Here comes the lawman, boy," Roper said. "Am I right?"

As the lawman appeared at the bottom step, the young man jerked his head in a quick nod.

"Okay," he said, then loud enough for the sheriff to hear, "thanks for the key."

13

Roper didn't get much sleep.

He stuck the wooden chair beneath the doorknob of his new room, set the pitcher and basin on the windowsill in case somebody tried to get in that way. Then he went to bed fully dressed with his gun beneath his pillow.

He dozed here and there, but was awake when first light came streaming through the window. He sat, his stomach growling. Killing two men had done nothing to ruin his appetite. They would have killed him for two bits, so they deserved what they got.

Roper didn't know if the desk clerk had told Nancy the saloon girl what had happened. He also didn't know how many other men she had on a string. The clerk was worried about getting killed, and Roper doubted the girl did her own killing.

He'd decided to stick to his plan about approaching the stockyard boys in the saloon, but that meant having it out with Nancy first. And lying awake that night, he had come up with an approach for that.

But first he wanted breakfast.

* * *

The café looked dubious from the outside, but Roper—as
"Andy Blake"—could not be choosy. Most of the clientele
was dressed as he was, so he went inside and got a table.
He ordered bacon and eggs, and resisted the urge to clean
the silverware while he waited. The waiter filled his coffee
cup before Roper could inspect it to see what was at the
bottom.

While he was eating breakfast, Sheriff Reynolds came
walking in. The lawman stopped inside the door, looked
around, spotted Roper, and walked over. Along the way,
longshoremen and stockyard worker averted their eyes, pre-
ferring not to attract the attention of the law.

"Mr. Blake," Reynolds said. "Mind if I join you?"

"You're the law," Roper said. "You ain't gonna harass
me, are ya?"

"That ain't what I'm here for," Reynolds said.

"Yeah, okay, sit down."

He didn't want to appear very comfortable talking to a
lawman.

"What's on your mind?" Roper asked.

"I checked at the stockyards," the lawman said. "You
ain't applied for a job."

"Did I tell you I did?"

"Yeah, you did," Reynolds said. "That's what you said."

"That ain't what I said," Roper replied. "I said I was
lookin' for a job and thinkin' about the stockyards."

"So where have you looked?"

Roper put his fork down and stared across the table at
the lawman the way a lot of men had stared at him in the
past.

"I'm gettin' my bearin's, Sheriff," he said. "You know a
man's gotta know where to drink and where to eat."

"This is the place you picked to eat?"

"Closest place to the hotel," Roper said. "How did you
find me here?"

"Like you said," Reynolds answered, "closest place to the hotel." He looked around. "And you fit in here."

The lawman had no idea what a compliment he had just played the disguised detective.

"You mind if I finish eatin'?" Roper asked. "I got a big day ahead of me."

"Big day of what?"

"Job huntin'."

Reynolds stood up.

"I'm gonna be keepin' my eye on you, Blake."

"Why? Because two jaspers broke into my room? How is that my fault?"

"Just a word to the wise," Reynolds said, and walked out.

As the lawman cleared the door, some of the other diners turned and looked at Roper, who contrived to look as if he was talking to himself, shaking his head and going back to his breakfast.

Most of the other diners went back to their meals, but two men seated together stood up and walked over to Roper's table, carrying their coffee cups.

"Mind if we join ya?" one of them asked.

Roper looked up at the two men. They were both in their thirties, with long, lank hair and the same rangy, saw-boned build. Roper quickly figured they were brothers.

"I don't know you," Roper said.

"Well, we can take care of that," the other one said. "I'm Stan Fixx and this is my little brother, Larry."

Larry, the "little" one, was actually a few inches taller than his brother.

"We heard you tell the law you're new in town, and lookin' for a job," Larry said. "We thought maybe we could help."

"Why would you wanna do that?"

"Well," Stand said, "anybody who's on the wrong side of the sheriff is okay with us."

"We just wanna welcome you to town," Larry said.

Roper looked up at the two men then said, "Yeah, okay, have a seat." He had expected to make contact with somebody in the saloon, not this morning in a café, but this could work.

"So, what did you do to get on the wrong side of Sheriff Reynolds?" Stan asked.

"Two fellas broke into my room last night," Roper said. "They were either gonna rob me or kill me."

"What happened?" Larry asked.

"I killed them."

"Lucky for you," Stan said. "Any idea who they were?"

"The sheriff recognized one of them," Roper said, "but I didn't get a name. Just some guy who bushwhacks men for their wallets."

Stan and Larry exchanged a glance.

"Mighta been somebody we know," Larry said.

Roper froze with his fork halfway to his mouth and said, "Not a friend, I hope. Or somebody you work with?"

"No, no, no," Larry said. "Hey, we're just a couple of guys who work in the stockyards."

"We heard the sheriff say you were lookin' for a job there."

"Yeah, maybe."

"Well," Stan said, "we could take you in there and introduce you."

"We got some influence."

"Yeah?" Roper asked. He pushed his plate away. "When could we do that?"

"Well . . . now, if ya want," Larry said.

"Yeah, we gotta go to work anyway."

"Sounds good," Roper said. "Let me pay my bill." He almost offered to pay for their breakfast, too, but caught himself. He was supposed to be somebody who didn't have much money.

The brothers pushed their chairs back and stood up.

"We'll just wait for ya outside," Stan said.

"Yeah, okay," Roper said, figuring they must have paid their bill already.

The Fixx brothers left the café and Roper called over the waiter to settle up.

"Did those two fellas pay their bill?" he asked.

"The Fixx brothers?" the waiter asked. "Oh, they never pay."

"Really. How do I get a deal like that?"

"You'd have to make arrangements with the owner," the man said, "like they did."

"Okay," Roper said, "maybe next time I come in."

The waiter nodded disinterestedly and walked away. Roper went out to meet the Fixx boys.

14

The brothers took Roper to the stockyards to the office of the foreman.

"What's this fella's name?" Roper asked as they walked up the steps.

"Pete Orton," Larry said. "Been the boss around here for a coupla years."

"A good boss?"

"He's fair," Stan said, "if you get on his good side."

"Like you boys?"

"Yeah," Larry said. "He likes us."

"Come on, we'll introduce ya."

Larry opened the door and the three men walked in.

There was a man sitting behind a large, raw wood desk. He had short hair, a lantern jaw, and the look of somebody who used to work in the stockyards before he became a foreman. In his fifties, he also had the look of a man whose muscle had started going to fat.

"What the hell?" he roared. "How many times I gotta tell you idiots to knock!"

"Oh, hey," Stan said, "sorry, boss."

"We got a feller here's lookin' fer a job, boss," Larry said.

"Yeah? I hope he ain't a friend of yours."

"Um, yeah, well, we just met this mornin'," Stan said.

"Yeah, at the café," Larry said. "The sheriff was givin' him a hard time."

"That a fact?" Orton asked. "What'd you do?"

"I killed two men."

Orton sat back in his chair and laughed.

"Where'd that happen?"

"My hotel room," Roper said. "Seems they thought I was asleep and decided to rob me."

"Only you wasn't asleep, huh?"

"Yeah, I was," Roper said, "but I'm a light sleeper."

"Haw," Orton laughed. "Light sleeper. I like that." He looked at the Fixx brothers. "You two, get lost. I'm doin' a job interview."

"Sure, boss, sure," Larry said.

"Get to work!" Orton said.

"Right, boss," Larry said. "See ya later, Andy."

"Yeah," Roper said.

The brothers left the office and Orton said, "Have a seat. Andy . . . what?"

"Andy Blake."

"From where?"

"All over."

"Where you from first, boy?" Orton asked. "You gotta answer my questions if you want a job."

"I'm from Missouri, originally," Roper said. "Been travelin' around. Came up here from South Texas."

"You wanted?"

"No."

"You sure you're not wanted somewhere?" Orton asked. "We can't hire no wanted men. If there's paper out on you, you better tell me."

"No paper," Roper said. "Not from anywhere."

"What can you do in a stockyard?"

"Anythin'," Roper said. "Cattle, sheep, whatever you got, I can tend 'em, haul 'em, butcher 'em."

"That so?" Orton said. "If that's true, you'd be pretty valuable around here."

"I figure."

"Yeah, you figure," Orton said. "I'm gonna have to talk to the sheriff about you before I hire you. And my boss."

"That's okay," Roper said. "The sheriff ain't gonna tell you nothin' against me."

"If he don't," Orton said, "then you'll be hired."

"When will I know?"

"Come back here in the mornin'," Orton said, "ready to work. If you're not hired, I'll let you know."

"Fair enough."

Orton stood up.

"You get the job we'll talk about salary tomorrow."

"Yes, sir," Roper said. "I appreciate that."

Orton shook hands with Roper, who then turned and left. He was pretty sure he'd be hired by the next morning.

Outside he found the Fixx boys waiting for him.

"What happened?" Stan asked.

"I'll find out tomorrow," Roper said, "but I'm pretty sure I got a job."

"Well, all right," Larry said, slapping Roper on the back. "We gotta have us some drinks later and celebrate."

"I'll be at the saloon," Roper said.

"Which saloon?"

"The Bullshead."

"That's a good place," Larry Fixx said. "We'll meet ya there."

"We gotta get to work before ol' Orton sees us out here," Stan said.

"I wanna thank you boys for the introduction," Roper said. "First round's on me tonight."

"Well, all right," Larry said, again. "See ya at the Bullshead."

15

Roper went back to his hotel, surprised at how well the day had gone so far. That is, for a day that started with him killing two men.

He sat down on his bed, trying to put everything in its proper perspective. Andy Blake was established with the law as a troublemaker, with the Fixx brothers as one of their own, with Orton as a possible employee. But he didn't know where he stood with Nancy the saloon girl. How would she take the fact that he'd killed two of her men? And who did she work for? He was going to have to go to the Bullshead and have a talk with her, find out if she was going to be sending any other boys after him. Or if her boss was.

He walked to his window and looked out. He was about to turn away when he saw Dol standing across the street.

"Damn it!" he said. He forgot about her. He still had to settle with her and get her out of town.

He left his room, went down the steps and outside the hotel to do just that.

* * *

"Don't be mad," she said as she saw him coming.

"Are you crazy?" he asked, barely containing his anger. "Do you want to get us killed?"

"I just want to do my part," she said. "I want to prove myself."

She was still in her disguise, with freshly applied soot on her face. Roper looked around. There was foot traffic around them, but nobody seemed to be paying them any special attention. Still, he had to get her off the street.

"Come on," he said, grabbing her arm roughly.

"Where are we going?"

"I don't know," he said. "Maybe I'll just take you to the train station and throw you on the first train that pulls in."

"Going where?" she asked, her eyes widening.

"It doesn't matter," he said, "Just away."

"Roper—" she said, but he cut her off.

"Don't call me that!" he said. "I don't want anyone to hear my name."

"Okay, okay," she said, "sorry. What name—"

"It's Blake, Andy Blake."

"Really?"

"What's wrong with that name?"

"It's kind of . . . plain."

As they walked, he asked her, "What are you calling yourself?"

"Jaime," she said.

"Jaime what?"

"I don't know," she said. "Nobody's asked me."

"How did you register at the hotel?"

She didn't answer.

"Oh no," he said. "Don't tell me you registered at the White Elephant under your real name?"

"I wasn't hiding from anyone," she said. "Not then."

"Damn it," he said. "Are you still there?"

"No, I checked out."

"Good."

"I checked into a cheaper hotel."

"Well, you're just going to have to check out again . . . Jaime."

She stopped walking abruptly. He took two more steps, then stopped and turned to face her.

"I'm not leaving!" she said firmly.

"Don't argue with me," he said. "Not here. Come on, we have to get out of Hell's Half Acre before somebody sees us together."

They walked until Roper felt they were in a sort of limbo, an area between Hell's Half Acre and the high-class saloons like the White Elephant and the Silverado.

He found a livery stable and dragged Dol to the back of it, so they could lean on the corral and talk away from prying eyes.

"What do I have to do to convince you?" he asked. "Physically put you on the train myself?"

He didn't want to do that. A man putting a writhing, squirming woman on a train would attract attention.

Dol became irritated, almost pugnacious, and suddenly looked comical behind the soot. Putting her fists on her hips certainly did not help matters.

"I don't know why I have to explain myself to you," she said.

"I'll tell you why," Roper said. "Because you're risking my life."

"I saved your life last night!"

"No you didn't," he said. "I was ready for those two, and I wanted one of them alive. All you did was get in the way."

"Well, fine, then," she said. "Fine. I can do this job without you."

"I'm warning you," Roper said. "If you stay in Fort Worth, stay away from me. You want to get yourself killed, that's one thing, but don't take me with you."

"Fine!"

She turned and stormed away from him. His preference certainly would have been to get her to go home, but the next best thing was for her to stay away from him. And—if she got herself killed—for him to feel no guilt at all.

None.

16

Roper went from his scene with Dol directly to the Bulls-head Saloon. In the middle of the day it was still crowded, with music and gambling going strong. Also, the girls were working the floor.

He stood just inside the batwings, trying to spot Nancy. When he didn't see her, he went to the bar and made a space for himself.

"What'll ya have?" the bartender asked.

"Beer."

"Comin' up."

Roper had stopped thinking about dirty glasses and silverware and rooms. If he was going to immerse himself in the character of Andy Blake, all of that was going to have to be accepted.

The bartender set a mug in front of him. It was surprisingly cold and good, with an impressive head on it.

"A nickel," the bartender said, "now."

Apparently, the bartender did not see in him whatever Nancy had detected the night before. The man took him at face value and wanted his money now.

Roper took out a nickel and slapped it down on the bar. The bartender picked up the nickel and walked away.

Roper nursed his beer, hoping Nancy would come out onto the floor eventually. When she hadn't shown by the time he finished his beer, he decided to take action. He waved the bartender over.

"I don't see that blonde around. You know, um . . ." he began.

"Nancy Ransom? She'll be on tonight," the bartender said.

"Uh, yeah, Nancy. Hmm," Roper said, "me and her, we was supposed to, uh . . ."

"She's upstairs, second door to the right," the bartender said. "If you're lyin', she'll put a bullet in ya. Good luck."

"Yeah, thanks."

The place was crowded and nobody was looking at him. It was too early for the Fixx brothers to come in looking for him. He walked casually to the open stairway and started up slowly, not wanting to attract any attention. When he got to the second level, he found Nancy's door and knocked.

"Who is it?"

He didn't answer, just knocked again.

"Whataya want?"

He knocked once more.

"Goddamn it . . ." she was swearing as she swung the door open. When she saw him, she froze in place. "You—" she started, but he cut her off by pushing her inside, and stepping in after her. He pulled the door closed behind him.

"Get out of here!" she snapped. She was wearing a dressing gown that was hanging open, revealing her undergarments and a lot of skin. Abruptly, she pulled it closed in front of her, crossing her arms. Her golden hair was piled atop her head, revealing a long, graceful neck.

"Relax," he said, "I ain't after your lily-white skin." He had to make sure he sounded like Andy Blake.

"If I scream, there'll be five guns in here in a minute," she said.

"I don't think you'll scream."

"Why not?"

"You ain't the type."

She snorted and said, "Type. So what are you supposed to be?"

"I'm just a guy lookin' for a job," he said. "I wanna know why you sent two guys to rob me, maybe kill me."

"What do you car—I don't know what you're talkin' about."

"Sure you do, honey," he said. "You made a quick decision about me yesterday, decided to send two of your cronies to rob me. What made you think I got anything worth robbing I don't know."

"Listen, honey," she said, with heavy emphasis on the word "honey." "I been here in the Half Acre long enough to know quality when I see it. And you know why?"

"Why?"

"Because I never see it," she replied. "Not in here."

She turned her back to him, belted her robe, then turned back.

"What are you talkin' about?" he demanded.

"You're a phony," she said. "I don't know what you're doin' here dressed like that, but you ain't lookin' for a job. At least, not for the same reason everybody else is."

"I don't know what you're talkin' about," Roper said. "All I want to do is get you to leave me alone."

"Hell, I ain't gonna bother you, cowboy," she said. "Why don't we agree to leave each other alone?"

"Fine. Just keep your men away from me," he said. "I don't wanna have to kill any more of 'em."

"Oh yeah," she said, still playing her part, "I heard about that. I heard some cowboy killed two bushwhackers. Good for you."

Roper stood there and stared at her. She wasn't going to admit she had anything to do with them. How, then, was he to believe that she'd leave him alone from this point on?

"Maybe I better talk to your boss," he said.

"The owner of this place?" Nancy said. "Why would he wanna talk to you?"

"Maybe he doesn't know you have a side job robbin' his customers."

Suddenly, Nancy became serious.

"You don't wanna be sayin' that out loud," she told him.

"Ah, I hit a nerve there, didn't I?" Roper said. "Your boss doesn't know. But you can't be doing this alone. You're either working for someone, or with someone."

She glared at him.

"What's your game?" she demanded.

"I thought we were talkin' about your game."

"You wanna talk to my . . . my partner?"

"That's right," he said. "I wanna get this cleared up."

"Well, you come back here tonight and we'll get it all cleared up."

"That's a deal," he said.

"Now get out!"

He tipped his hat, said, "Ma'am," and left.

17

Roper left the Bullshead, knew that he now had time to kill before he returned there to meet the Fixx brothers, as well as Nancy's partner.

He went back to his hotel to pick something up, then once again left the Half Acre neighborhood, walked past the White Elephant Saloon until he reached the new brick building that housed the Cattleman's Club of Fort Worth. Knowing he couldn't go in the front door looking the way he did, he went around to the back to look for another entrance.

He tried several doors, finding them locked tight, and was about to try a window when suddenly one of the doors opened. There was garbage outside the door, and a man came walking out carrying more. He was dressed all in white, and behind him Roper could see the kitchen. He headed for the door.

"Hey!" the man in white snapped. "You can't go in there."

Roper took ten dollars from his pocket and held it out to the man.

"You didn't see me."

The man looked at the money for a moment, then shrugged and said, "Have it your way, fella. I ain't seen ya."

Roper went into the building, made his way through the kitchen, with the kitchen staff giving him looks but not moving to stop him.

He came out of the kitchen into a long hallway and followed it until it emptied out into a foyer. Beyond him he could see men in expensive suits sitting and standing, holding drinks and big cigars. He couldn't afford to be seen by any of them but the one he was looking for.

He had a description—tall, white-haired, ruddy skin— but that fit more than one man. He finally decided he was going to have to spend a little more money, but if he did that, he might as well use the same man.

He went back to the kitchen to find the worker he'd already given money to.

"Hey," he said, waving the man over.

"Yeah?"

"You want to make more extra money?"

"Sure."

"I want you to find a man named Harold Kalish and bring him to me."

"I know Mr. Kalish," the man said. "He's very important."

"I know it," Roper said.

"Where should I bring him?"

"I don't know," Roper said. "I need to talk to him alone. Where can we go?"

"Wait, wait," the man said. "There's a meeting room in the back that's empty. Will that do?"

"That'd be great," Roper said. "Take me back there and then go get him."

"Gimme the money."

Roper handed him some more cash, and the man took him down another hallway to an empty room with a big meeting table in it, lined on all sides by chairs. The walls were paneled in brown oak that matched the table. As the kitchen worker went to get Kalish, Roper imagined that a lot of decisions affecting the cattle business in Fort Worth got made in this room.

That made it a fitting place for him to meet one of the men who had hired the Pinkertons.

18

When the door opened, one of the well-dressed, middle-aged men stepped in. He had a cigar in his mouth and a drink in each hand. He possessed a full head of gray hair, and a full beard.

"I assume you are Mr. Roper," he said.

"Yes, sir," Roper said. "It's a pleasure to meet you, Mr. Kalish."

Kalish crossed the room and handed Roper one of the drinks.

"I've been waiting for you to arrive," the man said with some disapproval.

"I've been here three days," Roper said. "Establishing my identity."

"Which is?"

"Andy Blake," Roper said, "stockyard worker."

"Have you gotten a job already?" Kalish asked.

"I should be hired in the morning," Roper said.

"Let's sit down," Kalish said.

They sat on opposite sides of the table from each other, and Roper told Kalish what had happened so far since his arrival.

"You killed two men?"

"They were trying to rob me in my room."

"So it doesn't have anything to do with the business at hand?"

"It has nothing to do with the reason I'm here, no."

"What else?"

"I'm taking steps to make sure nobody tries that again."

"Were you dressed like this?"

"I was."

"What made anybody think you had money?" Kalish wondered. "You're filthy. How did you get in here anyway?"

"Back door," Roper said, "through the kitchen."

"You're going to fit right in at the stockyards," Kalish said.

"Thank you, I'll take that as a compliment," Roper said. "Now look, I told the Pinkertons I'd make contact with you when I got here, but I can't do this again for a while. I can't take a chance that someone will see me coming here."

"But, Mr. Roper, I'll need reports—"

"No reports," Roper said. "I'll get in touch again when I have something solid to tell you."

"For the money I'm paying," Kalish said, "I'm just supposed to trust you?"

"Exactly," Roper said. "And I know you're not footing the entire bill. You just happen to be my contact here."

"Just happen to be?" Kalish asked, getting his back up. "I am your contact because I had a hundred head of cattle poisoned, right here in these stockyards. I had a man killed here."

"Tell me about that."

"It was made to look like he fell, and was trampled by the steers," Kalish said, "but I know better."

"Who was he?"

"Another man we hired," Kalish said.

"Another detective?"

"A stock detective, yes," Kalish said.

Roper sat back and took a drink. This was bad. He wasn't told that there had already been a stock detective killed on the job.

"Was it known that he was a detective?" he asked.

"No," Kalish said, "that never came out."

Which didn't mean that the men who killed him didn't know who he was.

"All right," Roper said, "I'm just going to have to be extra alert."

"For the money I'm paying, I would hope so," Kalish said.

"Speaking of which," Roper said, "I need some expense money."

"Expenses?" Kalish asked. "Like what?"

"For instance, I had to pay to get in here and see you," Roper said. "I've been paying out money since I got here, and I need a bit more."

He actually didn't need much more, but he found himself wanting to give this man a hard time.

"How much?" Kalish asked dubiously.

"How much you got on you?"

Kalish put his glass down, balanced his cigar on the edge of the table, and took out his wallet.

"I have several thousand dollars here."

Roper decided to take it easy on the man and said, "Just let me have a thousand."

"A thousand?"

"That's all."

Reluctantly, Kalish handed over the cash.

"That's all?" Kalish repeated. "Will I get receipts for the money?"

"Take that up with the Pinkertons."

Roper stood up and pocketed the money, then finished his drink.

"I've got to go."

"How do I get in touch with you?"

"You don't."

"What? Why not?"

"Let me ask you something first. What was his name? The other detective?" Roper asked the question hoping it wasn't somebody he knew.

"Henderson," Kalish said, "Walt Henderson."

Roper breathed a sigh of relief, then felt ashamed. He'd never heard of the man, but being relieved was not the way to react to his death.

"Did you have a way to get in touch with your other detective?"

"Yes, of course," Kalish said. "Henderson and I—we had a system—"

"And now he's dead," Roper said. "So no system, and no getting in touch with me. You'll just have to wait to hear from me."

Kalish stared at Roper, then said, "I just hope you are as good as the Pinkertons told me you are."

"Wait a minute," Roper said. "I was told you asked them for me."

"Well," Kalish said, "we asked about you, and they assured us as to your competence."

"Mr. Kalish," Roper said, "don't worry. I know my job."

"I hope so, Mr. Roper."

"Blake," Roper said, "the name's Andy Blake."

"Yes, of course," Kalish said, "Mr. Blake."

If the Pinkertons hadn't been involved, and if he hadn't already established his Andy Blake identity, Roper might have walked away from Harold Kalish right there and then.

"I'll be in touch," he said, and left the room.

19

Roper left the Cattleman's Club the same way he got in, through the kitchen. It was apparently Mexican food day, and on his way out, the kitchen worker he had paid to let him in handed him a taco.

"Thanks," he said.

He went out the back, eating the taco. He was angry, felt like sending William Pinkerton a telegram telling him to go to hell. There was no excuse for not telling him about the other detective. Not knowing could have cost him his life.

But he was into this now. There were people here who knew him as Andy Blake. Hell, there were people who had tried to kill Andy Blake. He'd put too much into this job already.

He finished the taco before he got to the street. It was pretty good. There was a clock tower across the street that told him it was midday. He still had some time before he had to go to the Bullshead. He decided to do some research.

Roper went to the offices of the *Fort Worth Star* and made arrangements to spend time in their morgue. A newspaper morgue had no bodies in it, just copies of old newspapers.

Roper spent the afternoon reading up on some of the problems the cattle business and the stockyards had been having over the past year. He also read where there was a faction in place who wanted to establish plants in town to butcher the cattle on-site, instead of shipping them out. It seemed like all the trouble began after that announcement had been made. Somebody, he thought, wanted to keep the business of butchering the cows out of Fort Worth.

Roper was about to quit and leave the morgue when he had a second thought. He sat back down and looked through the newspapers until he found the one that covered the death of the detective in the stockyards. The story did not mention that he was a detective, and did not refer to him by his real name, Henderson. It said simply that a stockyard worker named Gentry had fallen in the pens and been trampled to death by a herd of steers. Nothing was said about the death being suspicious. Roper looked further, but didn't find any other stories that matched the facts he'd been given by Kalish. This had to be the one. He filed the name "Gentry" away in the back of his mind, and this time he did leave the morgue, and the building.

Roper showed up at the Bullshead before dusk. It looked as if some of the stockyard workers had already joined the crowd, and the place was in full swing. Somebody was pounding on the piano badly, arguments were going on at the gaming tables, and the girls were expertly avoiding the groping hands of the customers, both sober and drunk.

He paused inside the batwings, looking around for the Fixx brothers, but didn't see them anywhere. Figuring they'd show up later, he made his way to the bar. It was not as easy as it had been earlier, but he finally managed to make a space for himself and get a beer. The bartender was not the same one he'd spoken to earlier about Nancy.

He turned his back to the bar and looked around, didn't spot Nancy working the floor. He decided to remain at the bar, making it easy for the Fixx brothers to find him when they arrived. Also, he'd be able to see the whole floor from there and would know when Nancy came down for work.

A paunchy man with gray stubble and a sweat-stained hat spotted Roper at the bar, crossed the room, and went up the stairs. Nobody paid him any mind as he got to the top and knocked on Nancy's door.

"Come!" she said.

He opened the door and entered, his hat in his hand.

"What is it, Weaver?" she asked. She was seated at her dressing table, applying her makeup.

"He's here."

She looked at him in the mirror.

"Are you sure?"

"You described him to me, Miss Nancy," he said. "It sure looks like him."

She stood up, grabbed a robe, and put it on over her gold-and-red gown. She crossed to the door, went outside, and managed to peer down at the bar without going right up to the railing. She saw Andy Blake standing at the bar with a beer in his hand, then she went back into the room. She removed the robe and sat back down at the dressing table. In the mirror Weaver could see the plunging cleavage of her gown and couldn't take his eyes off the pale globes of her breasts.

"All right," she said, reaching up to do something to her hair. The move made her breasts swell, almost spilling out of her dress. Weaver swallowed, wanted to look away, but could not. "Is Manko here?"

"Yes, ma'am."

"Point out Blake to him, and tell him it's time," she said.

"Yes, ma'am."

"And Weaver?"

"Yes, ma'am?"

"Tell him not to be stupid and try it alone," she said. "We want this to work."

"Yes, ma'am."

Weaver turned and moved toward the door.

"Weaver?"

"Yes, Miss Nancy?"

"Is Mr. Bonner in his office?"

"Yes, ma'am," Weaver said. "As far as I know."

"All right." She turned back to the mirror. "Get out."

"Yes, ma'am."

After he was gone, she sprayed some perfume in the air to dispel the scent of the old rummy, then went back to her makeup.

20

A few hours after speaking with "Andy Blake," Harold Kalish was sitting in a leather armchair in the Cattleman's Club, drinking brandy and smoking a fine cigar. The time of day was between lunch and dinner, and the room he was seated in—one of several such rooms in the building—was sparsely occupied. There were three other men seated, each alone, scattered about the room.

Kalish enjoyed this time of day. His business forced him to interact with others all day long, and he enjoyed moments like this, when he could sit alone and enjoy a drink and a good cigar without having to make conversation. He also enjoyed these moments because he knew they wouldn't last.

To illustrate that, another man entered, walked slowly around the room, then came over and sat across from Kalish. He was a portly man in his fifties, wearing a three-piece gray suit and sporting a potbelly, which caused his white shirt to show at the bottom of his vest. A waiter appeared immediately.

"Sir?" he said.

"What are you drinking, sir?" the man asked Kalish.

"Brandy," Kalish said.

"I'll have the same," the man told the waiter.

"Yes, Mr. Arnold."

As the waiter walked away, Adrian Arnold took a cigar from the box on the table next to him, snipped off the end with a tool he also took from the box, and then lit the cigar, drawing until he had the tip glowing properly. By the time he was done, the waiter had returned with his brandy.

"Thank you," Arnold said.

"You're welcome, sir."

The waiter withdrew.

Arnold sipped his brandy and said, "I got your message. You saw him?"

"Yes," Kalish said, "I saw him today. Just a few hours ago, in fact."

"Well, finally," Arnold said. "Did he say why he's late?"

"Actually, he's not late," Kalish said. "He's been in Fort Worth for three days, but he has spent that time establishing his identity."

"Which is?"

Kalish simply stared at Arnold, sucked on his cigar, and kept silent.

"Yes, all right," Arnold said. "I don't need to know that."

"I'm the one he's supposed to be in contact with," Kalish said.

"Right, right," Arnold said. "So, what did you think of him?"

"I can see why he and old Allan Pinkerton never got on," Kalish said. "He's his own man, doesn't kowtow to anybody."

"Is that good?"

"I think so," Kalish said. "I don't need a lot of 'yessir' and 'nosir.' I need a man who can get this job done."

"And can he?"

"He says he can," Kalish said.

"And you believed him?"

"Actually," Kalish said, "I did."

"And he's still in the dark about . . . certain things?"

"He's still in the dark," Kalish said, rotating his cigar in his mouth, "about certain things, and he has to stay that way."

"Of course," Arnold said. "As long as we get what we're paying for."

"Right."

"You send a telegram to Mike Hurley?"

"Not quite yet," Kalish said. "I thought we'd talk first."

"Well," Arnold said, "you better get that sent then. We want to make sure we keep the president of the Union Stockyard Company happy."

"Yes," Harold Kalish said, "yes, we do . . . very happy."

"These are desperate times, Harold," Arnold said. "I don't have to tell you that."

"No," Kalish agreed, "you certainly do not," but he doubted Arnold had heard him.

"We need to find whoever's behind all this bad business," Arnold went on, "before everything blows up in our faces."

"Don't worry, Arnold," Kalish said. "I truly believe Mr. Roper is the man for this job."

"Well, I hope you're right, Harold," Arnold said. "I certainly hope you're right."

21

Roper finished his first beer and got a fresh one. Still no sign of the Fixx brothers, or Nancy. He was considering going up to her room again when somebody jostled his arm, and he spilled beer on himself.

"Hey, watch it, friend!"

He turned to look at the man who had bumped into him. He was big, over six feet, wearing trail clothes and a gun on his hip. Not a stockyard worker, because from what Roper had been able to see so far, they didn't wear guns.

"Whatsamatta, Manko?" another man asked.

"This feller bumped me," Manko said, "got beer on me."

Roper studied the man, didn't see any wet drops on him.

"Looks to me like I got the worst of it, friend," Roper said. "Sorry."

He turned to put the mug on the bar so he could dry himself off when the man, Manko, did it again. This time the bump was obviously deliberate.

"Goddamnit, ya did it again!" Manko swore.

"Now, look," Roper said. "I don't know who put you up to this—"

"You bumped inta me!" the big man snapped.

"I think it was you who bumped into me," Roper said, "and on purpose. Now what's your game? Who put you up to this?"

"You callin' me a liar?" Manko asked.

"He called ya a liar, Manko," a third man said from down the bar. "I heard him."

"Me, too," said the second man.

Three of them, Roper thought, at least. First they sent two after him, now three. Unless there were more in the crowd.

This had to be Nancy's work. She knew he was coming back. She must have set this up.

"Now look, friend—" Roper started, but the big man wasn't having any of it.

He put his big paw on Roper's chest and pushed.

"I think I need ta teach you a lesson," Manko said.

Normally, Roper would have tried to talk his way out of this, but now he was forced to act as Andy Blake would.

Before he could move, though, Manko grabbed the glass of beer and dumped the contents on Roper's shirtfront. It dripped down and wet his trousers as well.

"Hey, look, Manko," the second man said, "it looks like he wet hisself."

"Yeah," the third man said, "you scared him so bad, he wet himself."

Damn it, Roper thought, but it was Andy Blake who threw the punch.

Roper was wearing a gun, as were the other men, but it did not occur to him to draw it. This did not yet seem to him to be a life-or-death situation. It seemed as if they were simply goading him into a fight, and Andy Blake certainly would have been goaded.

His punch landed solidly, dead center on the big man's face. His nose exploded and blood poured down the front of his shirt, but he did not go down. Instead, he threw a punch of his own that landed on Roper's jaw. The disguised detective was rocked back. He would not have gone down, though, except for the fact that he tripped on someone's foot. Later it would seem to him to have been deliberate, but at the moment he was only concerned that he was going down. He'd seen a lot of men kicked when they were down. It just seemed to invite it, and often it resulted in someone dying, sometimes by accident, and sometimes on purpose.

He looked up and saw the big man, Manko, bleeding profusely from the nose, and his two cohorts both coming toward him with bad intentions.

He knew the kicks were coming . . .

Nancy could hear the commotion from her room as the piano had stopped. She came out of her room, went right to the railing, and looked down at the saloon floor. The action there centered on the bar, where moments before Andy Blake had been standing.

Satisfied, she went back into her room and closed the door.

Manko and his friends were preparing to launch their kicks at Roper when the batwings opened and the Fixx brothers entered. They noticed the action right away, and saw Roper on the ground.

"Fight!" Larry shouted.

"Come on!" Stan yelled.

They charged the bar and bulled into Manko and his friends before they could land their kicks.

Roper scrambled to his feet, and suddenly the fight was three-on-three . . .

Roper knew he could not go toe-to-toe with Manko. The man was simply too big. And so far no one had gone for their guns, which was good, since the Fixx boys weren't wearing any. And no one else joined in, which left the fight three-on-three.

Manko threw a vicious punch at Roper, which he ducked. Missing threw the big man off balance, and Roper took the opportunity to kick one leg out from under him. The big man went down hard. Roper looked over at the Fixx brothers, and they were handling their opposition pretty easily. He saw them each land several punches, and their opponents went down.

Roper turned just as Manko came to his feet and charged him. He sidestepped the man, putting both hands out to push him as he went by, so that he went into the bar headfirst with considerable force.

Suddenly, it got quiet.

Stan and Larry Fixx came over to stand by Roper, who was looking down at Manko. The man's head had cracked the wood of the bar, and he was lying there, stunned. They could all have stomped him if they'd wanted to. Instead, Roper turned to the brothers.

"You guys got here just at the right time," he said. "Saved my bacon."

"What was that all about?" Stan asked.

"I don't kn—" Roper started, but looking past the brothers, he saw one of the fallen men get to his knee and draw his gun. Roper pushed Stan Fixx out of the way, drew his gun, and fired. The bullet hit the other man in the shoulder, and he dropped his gun.

"No guns!" Roper yelled. "This was just a brawl. No need for guns."

Manko rolled over, blinked, then waved an arm and shouted, "No guns!"

The second fallen man took his hand away from his gun. The first man was clutching his wounded shoulder.

Roper holstered his gun, then reached down and helped Manko to his feet.

"I think," he said, "we should all have a beer before the sheriff gets here. We're going to have a lot of explaining to do."

"Step right up, boys," the bartender said, putting beers on the bar. "On the house!"

22

Sheriff Reynolds arrived moments later, had a free beer, then marched all the combatants over to the jail for a conversation. He put them all in cells, except for the one who had been shot—he went to the doctor's office—and then took them out one at a time to question them.

He was talking to Manko, which left Roper alone in the cell blocks with Larry and Stan Fixx, and the third man in Manko's group.

Roper was in one cell with the Fixxes, while the other man was in the next cell. Roper went to the bars that separated them.

"Hey."

"Yeah?" the man asked. He was lying on the bunk with one arm across his eyes.

"What's your name?"

"Riggs."

"Riggs," Roper said, "what was that all about?"

"Hell if I know."

"Well, what did Manko tell you?" Roper asked. "Hell, I don't know any of you."

Riggs dropped his arm from his face and looked at Roper.

"Friend," Riggs said, "all I know is Manko said Miss Nancy told him to rough you up. He offered us fifty dollars each to help him."

"That was it?"

"That's all I know."

"Was he told to kill me?"

"If he was, he didn't tell us."

"Your buddy went for his gun."

"Dolan's an idiot," Riggs said. "That was his own idea."

"I see."

"You coulda killed 'im," Riggs said. "Why didn't you?"

"What makes you think I wasn't trying?"

"The way you handled that gun," Riggs said. "You were three feet away. You coulda killed him."

"I'm not lookin' to kill anybody," Roper said in Andy Blake's voice. "I just wanna be left alone."

The sheriff came in with Manko, then put him in with Riggs. The big man wasn't breathing real well through his mashed nose.

"I need a docta," he said mushily.

"Yeah, yeah," Reynolds said, "after he gets that bullet outta your friend's shoulder."

"Blake," he said, "you're next."

Reynolds opened the door and Roper walked out, waited while the sheriff locked it again.

"Siddown," Reynolds said, "and tell me what the hell happened."

"Damned if I know," Roper said. "The big fella came over and started a fight with me. Him and his friends were about to stomp me when the Fixx brothers came in and saved my ass."

"Just like that?" Reynolds asked. "Why would they do that?"

"We met yesterday."

"And now you're friends?"

"Looks like."

"And what about Dolan?"

"Who?"

"The man you shot."

"He was about to backshoot one of the Fixx boys," Roper said. "I stopped him."

"Yeah, you did," Reynolds said. "Way I hear it, you stopped him slicker'n snot."

"I got lucky."

"So you ain't a gunhand?"

Roper snorted. "Not hardly."

Reynolds regarded Roper suspiciously.

"You already killed two men since you've been in town," he said finally, "and now this. What am I supposed to think, Blake?"

"Think what you want, Sheriff," Roper said. "I came here to try and get a job. Before I know it, somebody's trying to rob me, and somebody else is pickin' a fight. Now, I don't look for trouble, but I don't back away from it neither."

"No, you sure don't."

Reynolds sat there, looking at Roper and frowning. For just a moment the detective had the urge to confide in the lawman, but it passed quickly. He never even considered telling the man what Riggs had told him about Nancy. He was going to have to take that up with the woman himself. And somewhere away from the Bullshead. He wasn't going to try that again.

"All right," Reynolds said.

"All right, what?"

"Your stories match," the lawman said.

"What did Manko say?"

"That you bumped into him," Reynolds said, "and you say he bumped into you. The Fixx boys say they came in, saw you in trouble, and helped out."

"What about Riggs?" Roper asked. "What did he say?"

"That his friend's an idiot, and went for his gun," Reynolds said. "He doesn't know why you didn't kill him."

"I don't wanna kill anybody, Sheriff," Roper said. "I just wanna make a livin'. Why can't anybody understand that?"

Reynolds took Roper's gun from his drawer and handed it over.

"What about the Fixx brothers?"

"I'm lettin' them out," he said.

"And the others? Manko? Riggs? Dolan?"

"They'll stay in jail overnight," Reynolds said. "Seems to me they started it."

Roper strapped his gun on as the sheriff made for the cell blocks. He stopped before entering.

"One other thing."

"What's that?"

"I talked with Pete Orton," Reynolds said. "I gave you a clean bill of health, so he's gonna hire you tomorrow."

"Thanks for tellin' me that."

Reynolds pointed a finger at Roper and said, "Don't make me sorry I did that."

"I won't."

23

Roper stepped outside the sheriff's office with Stan and Larry Fixx.

"Come on, let's get a drink," Stan Fixx said.

"Not at the Bullshead," Roper said.

"Naw," Larry Fixx agreed. "We'll go someplace else."

"You fellas lead on," Roper said. "I'm the new guy in town, remember?"

"Yeah, well, for a new guy," Stan said, "you ain't makin' friends real quick."

"Those guys?" Roper said. "No friends of mine."

"Why'd they start a fight with you?" Larry asked.

"Ya got me," Roper said. "Maybe it was *because* I'm the new guy in town."

As they walked away from the sheriff's office, Stan said, "Manko's for hire, Andy."

"That's right," Larry said. "Somebody sent him after you."

"Well," Roper said, "I ain't got any idea who would do that."

"Maybe the same person who sent those other two men after you," Stan said. "The ones you killed."

"When you got on the wrong side of the sheriff," Larry added.

"Could be," Roper said. "But I sure as heck don't know why."

"Come on," Stan said, "there's a small saloon around this corner."

"I just want one beer to wash away the taste of that cell," Roper said, "and then I gotta turn in. The sheriff told me he talked to Pete Orton and he's gonna give me the job tomorrow."

"One drink it is, then," Larry said, "to celebrate our new coworker."

"What are you gonna be doin'?" Stan asked.

"I don't know," Roper said. "I told him I can do about anythin'."

"And is that true?" Larry asked.

"Pretty much."

"Well," Stan said, "I guess we'll find out tomorrow."

They stopped in front of the Ace High Saloon, a much smaller place than the Bullshead, which offered whiskey and beer but no gambling.

Which suited Roper.

After the one promised beer with the Fixx boys, Roper tried to wish them good night. But they wouldn't leave him alone.

"You get in trouble too easy, boy," Stan said.

"We're gonna walk you to your hotel and tuck you in," Larry said. "We don't want you gettin' yerself killed before you can start yer new job."

"Well, much obliged," Roper said, because he knew he'd never talk them out of it.

When they reached his hotel, Stan Fixx said, "Shitfire, boy, no wonder you almost got killed. This ain't no place for a workin' man to be stayin'."

"It's fer workin' girls," Larry said.

"It's cheap," Roper said.

"Well, tomorrow mornin' you check out," Larry said. "We got a place you can stay that's cheap, and a helluva lot cleaner than this place."

"You boys are really takin' me under your wing," Roper said.

"Hey," Stan said, "we don't forget you saved one of us tonight. That jasper was gonna plug me."

"An' you plugged him," Larry said. "We don't really know which one of us he was gonna shoot, so I figure you saved both of us."

"I'll see you boys tomorrow, then," Roper said.

"We'll be right here bright and early, waitin' for ya," Larry said.

"We'll take you to a good place for breakfast."

"Good night," Roper said, wondering if he was ever going to be able to get away from his new friends to do his job.

His real job.

Nancy heard about what had happened in the Bullshead when she came down to work, and she wasn't happy. The man closest to the action—the bartender—gave her most of the information.

"It was odd," he said, "but Manko and his boys seemed real determined to get into a fight with this fella. If those Fixx brothers hadn't come in when they did, they prolly woulda stomped him to death."

"What about the shooting?"

"One of Manko's friends went for his gun," the barman said. "That fella Blake outdrew him slicker'n spit."

"Is he a gunhand, do you think?"

"He don't look like one," the bartender said, "but he handled that gun okay."

"Where are Manko and his boys?"

"In jail overnight, way I hear."

"Yeah, okay," Nancy said. "Thanks." She turned and saw her boss at the Bullshead, Aaron Bonner, coming toward her. Bonner was a small, dapper man in his forties who had run many businesses in the East, and then came west to Fort Worth specifically to buy and run a saloon and gambling hall. He was, however, disappointed to have found the only one available located in Hell's Half Acre, but decided to buy it anyway. The place had been called something colorful when he bought it, but he changed the name to the Bullshead.

"Nancy, what the hell," he said.

"Just a little excitement, Aaron," she assured him. "It didn't distract anyone from the gambling."

"This is why I've got to get a bid in on the White Elephant."

"Is it up for sale?"

"That's what I hear."

"That would be fabulous."

He rubbed her arm and said, "And I'd be taking you with me . . . though none of these others."

"I don't blame you," she said. "That place reeks of class."

"No nightly shootouts there, I'm sure," Bonner said.

"Not that I know of."

Bonner looked around, satisfied that things had gone back to normal.

"All right, then," he said. "I'll be in my office. Come in later and give me a report, will you?"

"The night's almost over," she told him.

"I know," he said. "Just do it, okay?"

"Whatever you say," she replied. "You're the boss."

He touched her arm again, rubbed it, and said, "Remember that."

She fought the urge to recoil from his touch and said, "I will."

He nodded, turned, and walked back to his office.

Nancy turned to the bartender and said, "I need a whiskey."

24

Roper found the Fixx brothers waiting for him outside the hotel the next morning.

"Hey, you're nice and early," Larry said. "We got us an hour before we gotta start work."

"Did you check out?" Stan asked.

"I did."

"Where's yer things?"

"All I got's in here," Roper said, indicating the saddlebags over his shoulder.

"Well," Larry said, "you'll have to buy some work clothes after you get yer first pay."

"I figured that."

"Let's get some breakfast," Stan said. "We can talk more over eggs."

"Sounds good to me."

The café the two brothers took him to was slightly better than the other places he had eaten while in Fort Worth. It was located about halfway between the hotel and the stockyards.

"After work we can take you to a rooming house run by a widow lady," Stan said. "She rents rooms out cheap to fellas who work the stockyards."

"Her husband worked there until he died," Larry said. "She likes to take care of the boys."

"That sounds right nice."

They all had bacon and eggs, a little greasy, but edible. Around them it looked like most of the diners were also stockyard workers. The Fixx boys seemed to know everyone, and they made a few introductions.

When breakfast was over, they left the café and walked to the stockyards.

"We have to get to work," Larry said, "but you better report to Orton."

"Hey," Roper asked, "what is it you guys do?"

"We're wranglers," Stan said.

"Somebody's gotta push those big beasts around," Larry said.

Well, they certainly seemed big enough to do that job adequately.

"I'll see you guys later," Roper said. He went up the stairs to the office door, remembered to knock before entering.

"Blake," Orton said from behind his desk, "have a seat."

Roper sat down.

"I have a favor to ask," Orton said.

"A favor?"

"You strike me as being a lot smarter than these others."

"What others, sir?"

"The rest of the men who work for me," Orton said. "Like the Fixx boys."

Roper started to speak, but Orton cut him off.

"Don't get defensive," Orton said. "I know you and the boys have a friendship. They're good workers, but they're not very smart. You are."

Roper was starting to think he was going to have to work on his undercover skills.

"Sir," Roper said, "I'll do whatever job you assign me."

"I'd like you to work with me," Orton said.

"Sir?"

"I need somebody right in here," Orton said, "and somebody who can work auctions with me."

"I'm not an auctioneer, Mr. Orton."

"Stop calling me sir and Mr. Orton," Orton said. "Just call me Pete. Or boss, if you want."

"Okay, boss."

"I don't need an auctioneer, I need somebody to work behind the scenes," Orton said. "Somebody who can read and write. You can read and write, can't you?"

"I can."

"And can you do math? Sums?"

"Yes, I can."

"Then I'd like you to take a clerk job," Orton said. "It'll keep you from having to work with the cows, keep you out of the manure. Whataya say?"

Roper hesitated, then said, "I say okay."

"Good." Orton opened his top drawer, took out a brown envelope, and handed it across the desk.

"What's this?" Roper asked.

"Expense money. I need you to get cleaned up, get a haircut and a shave, and buy some new clothes."

"Is this an advance on my salary?"

"No, that's company money," Orton said. "If you're gonna work with me, you need to be presentable. Get it done and come back after lunch, ready to work."

Slightly bemused, Roper stood and said, "Okay. You're the boss."

Outside it occurred to Roper that a haircut and a shave would divest him of a good portion of his disguise. But since he had a good week's growth on his face, he decided to keep the mustache.

So far during his time in Fort Worth, two people had judged him to be something other than what he was striving to appear to be. Nancy thought he was more, and Orton thought he was smarter. But at least Orton was not sending men after him to hurt or kill him.

He went in search of a barber.

* * *

After getting his shave and haircut, he checked his reflection in the mirror. The haircut had managed to get rid of most of the gray in his hair. The same could be said for the shave, but at least the mustache had some gray in it.

From there he went to a nearby mercantile to look at clothes. He knew Fort Worth had some actual men's clothing stores, but he didn't want anything too fancy. He assumed his boss simply wanted him to wear clean clothes. Besides, he didn't want to go to the higher-class parts of town. He had to maintain his cover, even though two people were acting as if they'd already seen through it.

25

Nancy Ransom left her room at the Bullshead and used a side door to leave the building. She didn't want to be seen leaving by anyone whether it was inside or out.

When she got to the main street, she walked quickly, keeping close to the buildings. She went three blocks and then turned right. She stopped at the first building she came to, went up the stairway that ran up the side of the building, and knocked on the door. When it opened, she stepped inside quickly.

"I was wonderin' when you'd show up," Eddie Parker said, closing the door.

"Things have been happenin'," she said.

"I thought maybe you didn't want your cut."

"Oh, I want it."

He laughed, walked to a chest of drawers, and opened the top one. He took out a small pouch and handed it to her. She hefted it, then tucked it into the purse she was carrying. As always, she tried not to stare at his huge ears.

"You better go over to the sheriff's office today," she told him.

"What for?"

"Manko's there," she said. "In a cell with Riggs and Dolan."

"What happened?"

"They tried for that stranger again."

"The one who killed Giles?"

"That's right."

"What happened?"

"He got in a fight with the three of them. A couple of stockyard workers stepped in and helped him. Then he shot Dolan."

"Dead?"

"No, he shot him in the shoulder. But the sheriff kept the three of them in jail—overnight, I guess. Maybe they need to be bailed out."

"Why should I bail 'em out?" he asked. "I ain't spendin' my money on your mistake. Why'd you send them after him?"

"There's something off about him."

"Then leave 'im alone," Parker said. "The way you described him, he don't sound like he's got enough money to make it worth our while."

"Maybe not," she said, "but . . . I don't know. He's just . . . wrong."

"Well, take my advice, Nancy," he said. "Leave 'im be. We got a good thing goin' here with you pointin' out our marks and me pickin' out the boys to send after 'em. Let's just both keep doin' our jobs."

"I suppose."

"And if you want them three bailed out, you're gonna have to do it yourself."

She studied Parker for a moment. He was in his late forties, had been walking on the wrong side of the law for years, but never anything big. He'd never been to jail. He knew when to act and when to wait. Maybe she should take her clue from him and leave that fellow alone.

"All right," she said. "Thanks for my cut."

He opened the door for her and said, "You sure you don't wanna stay and have a drink?"

"It's a little early for me, Eddie."

"We could skip the drink," he said hopefully.

She had never gone to bed with him, and never would. That would be mixing business with pleasure.

"Some other time, Eddie," she said, like always.

"Yeah," he said, and closed the door.

26

Roper came out of the mercantile with a package of new shirts under his arm. There was also a new pair of trousers in there. He started to cross the street when he saw Nancy coming around the corner. He ducked back, but she hadn't spotted him.

He watched her walk by, thought about following her, but if she was going back to the Bullshead—and she was heading in that direction—it wouldn't do him any good. He stepped out and walked after her, increasing his speed as he went. When he grabbed her arm and turned her around, she looked annoyed, but not frightened.

"You!" she said.

"Me."

"What do you want?"

"I wanna talk to you," he said.

"If you don't let go of my arm, I'll scream."

"We're in Hell's Half Acre," he said. "What's anybody gonna do?"

She glared at him.

"All right," she said, "but not on the street."

He looked around, saw a sad-looking café across the street.

"There," he said.

"That dump?"

"We don't have to eat there," he said. "I just wanna talk."

"Let's go to the Bullshead."

"No," he said, "I'm not havin' you sic any more of your friends on me."

She frowned, then said, "Okay, just let go." He did, ready to grab her again if she ran, but she didn't. They walked across the street and stepped into the café. The sixtyish owner looked shocked that anyone would walk in.

"We just want coffee," Roper said to him.

"Fine, fine," the squat little man said, just happy he had some customers.

The place was completely empty, so Roper grabbed a table for two against the back wall.

"Sit," he said.

For a moment he thought she'd bolt, but she relented and sat.

"What do you want?" she asked.

"I wanna know why you sent Manko and his friends to start a fight with me last night," he said. "I almost had to kill one of them."

"It was a mistake," she said.

"I'll say," he replied, "but why?"

"Look," she said, "it's just all been a mistake. It won't happen again."

"You're not answerin' my question," he said.

The owner came with a pot of coffee and two cups. He poured for them, then stood with his hands clasped and asked, "Anything else?"

"No, that's fine," Roper said.

The man withdrew.

"What is it about me that sent you after me?" he asked.

Nancy studied him for a moment, then said, "You're wrong, mister. I been in the Half Acre, and places like it, for a lot of years. You don't belong here."

"I don't disagree with you," he said, "but I ain't got the money to go anywhere else."

"Well," she said, "I guess that makes two of us."

Now it was his turn to study her.

"You know," he said finally, "I don't think it's the money that keeps you here. For you, it's somethin' else."

"There!" she said, pointing at him, her eyes flashing with something—not anger, but something else.

"What?" he asked.

"That comment right there," she said. "That's what I mean about you not belonging here."

She stood and started to leave, but he caught her arm.

"Do us both a favor," she said, yanking her arm from his grasp. "Stay away from the Bullshead. Stay away from me. Do whatever it is you came here to do, and get out of Fort Worth."

"Nancy—"

He stood up, but she rushed to the door and ran out.

He sat back down, thought about the exchange, and decided she was probably right. He should get on with his business and forget about her. Providing, of course, that she did the same thing and didn't send any more men after him.

The owner came over and said, "Pretty girl."

"Yes, she is."

"She didn't drink her coffee."

"No," Roper said. He picked up his cup and took a sip, then another one. He looked up at the man in surprise. "This is damned good."

"Hmph," the man said, tapping his chest with his hand, "you think I don't know that?"

27

Roper finished the surprisingly good coffee and vowed to go back there to try the food. He stepped outside and glanced in the direction Nancy had come from. He walked that way and looked around the corner. Buildings on either side. She could have come out of any of them, or none of them.

The purse she'd been carrying had been swinging heavily. A gun? he wondered. Or a poke? Maybe she had just come from seeing her partner, getting her cut of the bushwhack money?

She'd headed back in the direction of the Bullshead. He had to figure she was going back there. He had no more time to spend on her, though. He had to get back to work so he wouldn't get fired on his first day.

He tucked his package under his left arm, keeping his right arm—his gun hand—free. Maybe she intended to leave him alone from now on, but there was no point in taking any chances.

When he went back to work, Orton told him to go into the storeroom and change into his new clothes. After he came back out, the man started to educate him about the paper-work that needed to be done. He had even brought in a desk for Roper to sit at.

During the course of the day, Roper realized that Orton was constantly on call. Men would come running in with something demanding his attention, and at times his actual presence. At one point he ran out with a man, and when he came back, his boots were coated with manure.

Before going into the water closet to wash them off, he told Roper, "This is the kind of job I'm gonna want to del-egate to you eventually."

"You expect to have a lot of confidence in me," Roper observed.

"I hope to," Orton said. "I'm hoping that I'm right about you and you're as smart as I think you are."

"I hope so, too," Roper said.

Orton went to clean his boots. Roper took the opportunity to go to the man's desk and riffle it, in a controlled manner so that nothing would seem amiss. By the time Orton came back out, wiping his hands on a towel, Roper was back at his own desk, no wiser. He'd found nothing revealing on Orton's desk.

If somebody was sabotaging the operations in the stock-yards, no one was in a better position to do that than Orton himself. He was Roper's first suspect.

But given the number of men who worked in the stock-yards, who inhabited Hell's Half Acre, and Fort Worth in general, he was the first of many.

At the end of the day, the Fixx brothers came by the office to meet him. As he came down the steps, and saw them standing there, grinning happily, he knew he had to look at them as suspects, too.

"Hey, how was your first day?" Larry asked.

"Look at your new clothes," Stan said.

"It went okay," Roper said.

"Let's get a drink, huh?" Stand said.

"Sure," Roper said. "Let's go."

"But not the Bullshead, right?" Larry asked, slapping Roper on the back.

"Yeah, that's right, boys," Roper said. "Not the Bullshead."

The Fixx brothers took Roper to a saloon just outside Hell's Half Acre called Sullivan's. The difference a few feet made was amazing. The place was clean, with high ceilings, honest games, pretty girls, a good piano player, and cold beer.

They stood at the bar with their beers, and nobody jostled Roper's arm, on purpose or otherwise.

"So how'd the first day go?" Larry asked.

"How you like bein' Orton's clerk?" Stan asked.

"The day went fine," Roper said, "and it's better than bein' knee deep in cow manure all day. You boys stink."

"That ain't manure," Stan said. "That's how Larry smells all the time."

"Fuck you," Larry said good-naturedly.

"That why all the girls are stayin' away from us?" Roper asked.

"Naw," Larry said, "they're stayin' away 'cause they don't wanna be seen with no stockyard clerk."

"Don't listen to him, Andy," Stan said. "He wishes he could work inside, and not with all the cows."

"I'm buyin' you boys another round," Roper said.

"Clerks," Stan said. "God love 'em!"

28

Roper was impressed by the Fixx brothers.

They didn't gamble because they knew they couldn't afford it. Each brother bought one round of drinks after Roper bought the first round, and then they went back to buying their own. The brothers apparently played and drank within their means, which made them more intelligent than Roper had originally thought.

Roper adapted the same outlook for Andy Blake. He nursed his last beer and stayed away from the gaming tables. He remained at the bar and talked with the brothers, and eventually brought the subject around to the problems that had beset the stockyards of late.

"It's almost as if we're cursed," Stan said. "Nothin' is going right. Equipment is failing, cows are dyin'—"

"Dying of what?" Roper asked.

"They don't know," Larry said. "We ain't on the inside, but we heard the vets are stumped."

"And I heard somethin' about somebody dyin'?" Roper said.

"Yeah, that new fella," Larry said. "He fell into the pens and somehow got trampled to death."

"The steers musta been scared ta death to do that," Stan said.

"He get on anybody's wrong side?" Roper asked.

"You mean did somebody kill 'im?" Larry asked.

"Maybe he was foolin' around with somebody's wife? Or girlfriend?"

"We didn't get to know him," Larry said. "He was quiet, kept to himself. But he didn't seem like that kinda fella."

Stan agreed. Roper wondered how the dead detective had expected to be able to do his job without getting to know the other workers.

"You know," Roper said, turning his own attention to that problem, "I gotta meet some of the other guys, too. I don't want them thinkin' I'm stuck up because I got made clerk."

"I got an idea," Stan said. "I know a place where some of 'em drink."

"Yeah," Stan said, "we can go over there and introduce you to some of the other boys."

"Good." Roper said. "Let's do it. Where is that place?"

"I think you heard of it," Larry said with a smile. "The Bullshead."

The Fixx brothers convinced Roper to go back to the Bullshead with them.

"We're always gettin' into fights in saloons," Stan said. "That don't mean we ain't good customers and we can't go back."

Larry reinforced Stan's statement, and Roper finally gave in. He didn't want them questioning why he didn't want to go back there. Plus, if most of the stockworkers were drinking there, that's where he had to go to meet them.

They entered the Bullshead and the smell hit him immediately. He hadn't noticed it last time. But coming there directly from Sullivan's, he could smell the difference. Stale beer, even staler sweat, and the cheap perfume the girls heaped on to combat the smells around them.

They went to the bar and ordered three beers from a bartender who was unfamiliar to Roper, which suited him. The Fixxes, however, knew him and introduced him to Roper as "Sandy."

When they had their beers, they turned their backs to the bar and Stan said, "There. That's a whole table of guys from work."

The table he was indicating was the table of workers Roper had initially picked out during his earlier visits to the Bullshead. Meeting Larry and Stan Fixx had saved him from having to find a way to introduce himself to them. Now the brothers were taking care of that.

"Hey, boys!" Larry yelled.

The six men looked up at Larry and five of them grinned. Roper noticed one man roll his eyes and look away.

"Meet Andy Blake," Stan said. "He's new. Andy, that's Benny Williams, Luke Taylor, Mark Brecker, Sam Ambler, and Lester Hayes. And that unpleasant-lookin' fella, that's Jerry Tucker." Stan lowered his voice. "He don't like us."

"Nobody likes you, Stan, or your brother," Jerry said. "They're just bein' nice to you."

Jerry was in his mid-thirties, was dressed better than the others, and projected an attitude that said he was better. He was also the only one in the group who was wearing a gun. Roper had decided that Andy Blake wouldn't be wearing a gun when he was at work, and since he had gone out right after work with the Fixx boys, he still didn't have one on. He did, however, have a two-shot derringer tucked into one boot, and a knife in the other.

"Don't listen to him," Mark Brecker said. "Pull up some chairs. Whatta they got you doin', new guy?"

"I'm workin' in Orton's office as a clerk," Roper said.

"How'd you manage that?" Luke Taylor asked.

Roper shrugged and said, "It was the job he offered me,

and I really needed a job. I was prepared to work knee deep in shit, but—"

"Hey, don't knock it," Benny Williams said. "If I could get out of the shit, I would."

"You were born for the shit, Benny," Jerry Tucker said, "like these boys."

"Fuck you, Jerry," Larry said.

"Watch how to talk to me, dummy," Jerry said. "I'm the one wearin' a gun, remember?"

"We'll take that gun away from you and stuff it up yer ass," Stan said.

"The other dummy speaks," Jerry said. "The Dummy brothers."

Larry made a move, but Stan put his hand on his brother's arm.

"Shut the hell up, Jerry," Lester Hayes said. "None of us know why you have to wear that gun anyway."

"Because I'm good with it," Jerry said.

"Ha," Larry said. "You wanna see somebody good with a gun, you shoulda seen what Andy did here last night."

"Larry," Roper said, "I told you I got lucky."

"If you're so good with a gun, why ain't you wearin' one?" Jerry asked with a sneer.

"Now that I've got my job," Roper said, "I don't have any need for a gun."

"But you needed it last night," Mark said. "Why would you come back here without it?"

"We went to a saloon right from work," Roper said. "I didn't know we'd end up here."

"If you're good with a gun," Jerry said, "you wear it."

"I'm not here to prove anythin' with a gun," Roper said. "I'm tryin' to make a livin'."

"Ain't we all?" Sam asked, speaking for the first time.

Most of the men were in their late thirties or early forties, but Sam. He looked to be fifty or so, but he had big beefy shoulders and arms and certainly looked like the kind of man who could push cows and steers around.

They all had another drink and managed to direct the conversation away from Jerry's gun.

Jerry didn't take part in much of the conversation, and Roper really couldn't see why he was sitting with the group. For that reason he stuck out to the detective, which made him interesting when he was looking for a suspect.

He was going to have to check out Jerry Tucker.

29

Roper woke the next morning in a feather bed in Mrs. Varney's Rooming House. The Fixx brothers had been right about one thing: This place was much better than the hotel he'd been in.

He wanted to stay in the feather bed longer, but Mrs. Varney had warned him that if he missed breakfast, he'd have to eat out.

When he came down the stairs, dressed for work, Mrs. Varney's long wooden table was crowded with her boarders. There was, however, one spot left, and he claimed it.

"We got some new boarders this mornin'," Mrs. Varney said, "but I ain't got time to make introductions, so you boys better take care of it yourselves."

"Hi," the man on Roper's left said, "I'm Bill Catlin." He was in his forties, dressed like a businessman in a suit, although his jacket was hanging on the back of his chair.

"Andy Blake."

The man to his right was eating, and didn't bother to introduce himself.

The table was covered with plates of scrambled eggs, ham, potatoes, flapjacks, biscuits, and grits. Apparently, none of the other boarders—new or old—were interested in getting acquainted, so they all pretty much ate in silence. Roper found it odd. In other boardinghouses he'd usually found there'd be some drummer anxious to hawk his wares to the captive audience. Not the case here.

The food was excellent, and Mrs. Varney—all four-feet-ten of her—kept bustling in and out with even more food. The coffee was the best Roper had tasted in a while—well, since the day before in that café with Nancy. He still wondered why a place with coffee that good had been so deserted. Maybe the food didn't match. He still intended to go back and try it.

At one point he leaned over to Catlin and asked, "Is it always this quiet at breakfast?"

"Wasn't always," Catlin said. "We had a salesman with us last week, kept tryin' to sell us all new underwear at breakfast."

"What happened?"

"Somebody broke into his room, gave him a few whacks, and tore up his undies," Catlin said. "Since then nobody talks much."

"Probably wise," Roper said.

Catlin nodded and said, "I think so, too."

Mrs. Varney's three-story home was a virtual mansion, with the second and third floors turned into rooms for rent. The first floor had a sitting room and the large dining room they were eating in. The table was made of sturdy wood, about fifteen feet long, with a long bench on either side. Apparently, she wanted her boarders to eat and get out and not get comfortable. Roper's ass was already complaining about the hard wooden bench.

As Mrs. Varney came in and out through a swinging door, Roper could see the large kitchen. There was one other person in there, but he only caught a glimpse, as Mrs. Varney was the only one who ever came out. Roper assumed there were other rooms on the first floor, in the rear of the house, where Mrs. Varney lived.

One by one, the boarders finished eating, got up, and left.

Most of them looked like men who worked in town. One or two of them wore a gun and trail clothes, appearing to be men who were just passing through.

Eventually, it came down to Roper, Catlin, and two others at the opposite end of the table.

"How long have you lived here?" Roper asked him.

"A few months," Catlin said. "I'm tryin' to get myself established in town before I get a place of my own."

"What do you do?" Roper asked.

"I'm a lawyer."

"And these others?"

"Various jobs," Catlin said. "Several of the men work in the stockyards. Mr. Henry there, at the end, has a gun shop. He's talkin' to Mr. Avery, who works at the local apothecary. Others are just passin' through. Mrs. Varney doesn't discriminate. How about you?"

"Stockyards," Roper said.

"Really? You don't strike me as that kind of man."

"What kind of man do I strike you as?"

"Educated," Catlin said.

"Well," Roper said, "I just got the job yesterday. I'm clerking in the office."

"Ah," Catlin said, "that's more like it."

"What kind of law do you practice?"

"Whatever I can get, really," Catlin said. "Some estate work, an occasional criminal case. Came here from the East to get myself a more interesting life."

"How's it going so far?" Roper asked.

"Not much excitement, I have to admit," Catlin said. "But I'm hopeful."

"Seems I heard of some excitement here . . . what was it, last month? Fella died in the yards?"

"Yeah, but he just fell into a pen and got trampled," Catlin said. "Nothing there for a lawyer to get involved in."

"Unless he was killed."

"Well," Catlin said, slapping his napkin down on the table, "I didn't hear anything like that. I've got to get to my office. See you tomorrow morning."

"Sure."

Catlin left, and a few minutes later, the other two men did as well.

Mrs. Varney came out of the kitchen and looked startled to see him there.

"Still eatin', I see, Mr. Blake."

"Last one down, last one done, I guess, ma'am," he said. "The food was amazing."

"I have a good cook," she said, nodding.

"Well," he said, dropping his napkin on the table and standing, "I guess I'd better get to work. Don't want to be late on my second day."

Mrs. Varney nodded and started to clean up. She carried two armfuls of plates to the door and opened it with her ample behind. Roper caught a better, longer look at the kitchen, and the cook—a younger woman, very pretty, wearing an apron. She had long brown hair, held back in a long ponytail, and just for a moment their eyes met before the door swung closed.

30

Roper's first week at work was uneventful.

He was able to come up to speed fairly quickly on the way Orton did things, his filing system, his purchase orders, his personnel files. He even saw some ways he could have improved on everything, but he didn't want to seem that smart. All he was interested in was blending in, not standing out.

One of the surprises of his job was meeting his boss's wife, and that happened on the eighth day.

Orton had never even talked about his wife that week, and they had even eaten lunch together twice right there in the office.

On day eight, Orton was out in the yard when the door opened and a woman walked in. She was dressed simply, but expensively, in a brown fringe skirt, tan blouse, and black boots. Her auburn hair was worn long and she appeared to be in her mid-thirties.

"Can I help you, ma'am?" he asked.

She turned her head to look at him, stared a bit too long, appraising him.

"You look interesting," she said. "When did you start working here?"

"A week ago."

"I guess I should come around more often," she said, her tone overly flirtatious.

"Are you lookin' for Mr. Orton?"

"I am," she said. "Is he around?"

"He's out in the pens," Roper said.

"Oh, that's fine," she said. "I suppose I can look forward to him coming home smelling like manure."

"Comin' home?"

She came close enough to Roper's desk to bump it with her hip.

"I'm Louise Orton," she said.

"His . . . daughter?" Roper asked.

"Why, how sweet," she said. "No, actually, I'm his wife."

"Oh," Roper said, standing quickly, "Mrs. Orton. I'm sorry, I didn't know—"

"Relax, Mr.—"

"Blake, ma'am," he said. "My name's Andy Blake."

"Well, Andy," she said, "from here, you don't smell like manure."

"Ma'am—" he said, but stopped short when she came around the desk to stand next to him. She leaned in close enough for her nose to touch his neck as she sniffed him.

"Nope," she said, "no manure."

Her perfume tickled his nose and he thought, under other circumstances, this little dance would have been enjoyable.

At that moment the front door opened and Pete Orton stepped in. Louise Orton turned her head to look at him, but made no move to back away from Roper, so he took the liberty of taking a couple of steps away from her.

"Louise," Orton said. "What are you doing here?" He didn't seem at all happy to see her, and also didn't seem to mind how close she had been standing to Roper.

"Why, looking for you, darling," she said, moving back

around to the outside of Roper's desk. "Your new clerk has been entertaining me while I wait."

Orton walked to his desk. He did, indeed, reek of manure. Roper could smell it from across the room. Orton dropped the papers he was carrying on top of his desk.

"What do you want, Louise?" he asked again.

"What do I usually want, my dear?" she asked. "I need some money." She looked at Roper. "He keeps me on such a short leash."

Orton scowled, took some money from his pocket, and held it out to her. She had to walk across the room to take it from him.

"I assume that will be enough?" he said.

"That should do it," she said. "I only need a few things."

"I'm busy," he said. "I'll see you at home."

She walked to the door, opened it, and said to her husband, "Don't overwork your handsome new clerk." Then she looked at Roper. "Good-bye, Andy. Thanks for keeping me company."

She left, pulling the door closed behind her, not quite hard enough to break the glass.

Orton sat down behind his desk, still scowling. He took a bottle of whiskey from the bottom drawer, along with two glasses.

"Join me for a drink, Andy," he said.

Roper walked over and accepted a glass from his boss.

"Mr. Orton," he said, "I, uh, I wasn't—"

"I know you weren't," Orton said. "The woman is a shark, Andy. You'd do well to steer clear of her—and not only because she's my wife."

"Yes, sir."

Orton downed his whiskey and poured two more fingers.

"And like I told you, don't call me sir, or Mr. Orton," he said. "Just call me Pete. Got it?"

"I got it, Pete." Roper drank his whiskey and set the empty glass down.

"No more for you," Orton said. "Back to work."

"Yes, sir."

Roper went back to his desk. Orton finished his second drink, then replaced the bottle and closed the drawer. He went into the water closet for a short time and came out smelling only slightly less of manure.

Roper waited half an hour before bringing up the subject of Jerry Tucker. He brought some paperwork over to the desk for Orton to peruse and sign. In just a week Roper had come to understand how mind numbing office work could be.

"Good," Orton said, looking the paper over. "Good." He signed it and handed it back.

"Pete, what can you tell me about Jerry Tucker?" Roper asked.

"Tucker," Orton repeated. "Tucker."

"Wears a gun when he's not workin'," Roper said. "Thinks he's pretty good with it."

"Oh, him," Orton said. "He's an idiot. He's going to get himself killed one day."

"Or somebody else."

"That's why you should stay away from him when he's drinking," Orton said.

"I intend to," Roper said, "but he seems to have it in for me because of what happened the other night in the Bullshead."

"How did he find out about that?"

"The Fixx brothers," Roper said, "they like to, uh, brag."

"Those two," Orton said, shaking his head. "Why would you make friends with them?"

"Well," Roper said, "for one thing they introduced me to you."

"You seem much too smart to be friends with them, Andy," Orton said.

"Everybody thinks I'm so smart," Roper said. "Why is that?"

"Oh, I don't know," Orton said. "Maybe we're just wrong."

"Yeah, that may be," Roper said, and went back to his desk.

"No, we're not," Orton said, standing up. "I can see that you're an educated man, Andy. Why don't you tell me where you got that education?"

"I got it by the seat of my pants," Roper said. "Travelin', lookin', and listenin'."

Orton eyed him for a moment, then said, "That might make sense."

Before he could decide whether it did or not, the door opened and a man came in. He was wet with sweat and looked as if he was covered with dirt—or manure—from the waist down.

"Problem, boss."

"What is it?" Orton demanded.

"You better come and look."

Orton hesitated, then turned and pointed a finger at Roper.

"Another month and I'm going to let you handle things like this."

As Orton followed the man out, Roper was thinking that in a month's time he hoped to be gone and done with this case.

31

When the last man entered the saloon, the leader yelled out to him, "Lock that door!"

"Yessir."

The last man locked the door, then walked to a chair and sat down. He was the sixth man in the room.

"I've called you all here," the leader said, "because we need to escalate our efforts."

"Huh?" one of the men, Cal Edwards, said.

"He wants us to try harder," another man, Nick Brady, said.

"We been doin' a lot of damage," still another man, Steve Wilson, said. "And that detective gettin' killed—"

"That was unfortunate," the leader said, "not necessary. But it still hasn't persuaded the Eastern interests to forget about Fort Worth as a place for them to invest. That means we need to redouble our efforts to make them see."

"Redouble?" said Edwards, who still didn't seem to quite understand.

"He means we need to try harder," Brady explained.

"Why don't he just say that?"

Edwards shrugged.

"So whatta you want us to do?" Wilson asked.

"Just be ready," the leader said. "We're coming up with a plan, and when we have it in place, we want you all to be ready to act."

"That's all?" said Wilson.

"That's it," the leader said. "For now. Thank you all for coming."

The men stood up, unlocked the front door, and left. The leader remained where he was until the saloon was empty. Then a door opened in another part of the room, and a second man entered. He was well dressed, holding a thick lighted cigar.

"What do you think?" he asked.

The leader turned his head.

"If you want this to work," he said, "we'll need better men."

"And?"

"And that will take more money."

The second man stood in thought for a moment, smoking his cigar, then said, "You'll have it."

32

Mrs. Varney understood that her boarders worked—most of them—so she laid dinner out at seven. Most of them should have been able to get home from work by then. If they missed a seven o'clock dinner, they were on their own.

Roper got home at six, went to his room, washed in a basin, and changed out of his "work clothes." Wearing a cotton shirt and Levi's, he pulled on the same boots, still with the derringer in one and the knife in the other. Then he went downstairs.

The table was set, but there was no food yet. He heard voices coming from the sitting room and went in there. He found five men, standing and sitting, split into two different conversations. This was the first time he'd actually gone into the sitting room to socialize before the evening meal so he didn't really know anyone except Catlin, the lawyer. He thought he recognized one man's face from the stockyards but didn't know his name.

En masse, they turned and looked at him as he entered.

"Ah, Mr. Blake," Catlin said. "Have a good day?"

"It was okay."

"I don't believe you know the other members of our group."

Catlin made quick introductions of the men in the room. Roper filed away their names, then concentrated on a man named Embry, Charlie Embry.

"Charlie, there, works at the stockyards," Catlin said. "You two must have seen each other."

"Sure," Embry said, approaching Roper with his hand out, "Orton's man, right? I've seen you going in and out of his office."

They shook hands.

"I've seen you outside," Roper said.

"Yes, well, I don't have many reasons to go inside," Embry said.

Roper frowned. He knew what Orton meant about knowing he was educated. He could see it in this man's eyes, in his speech. Why was he working in the stockyards?

"You work the pens?" Roper asked.

Embry nodded and said, "And I like it. I'd rather work outside than inside."

"I know what you mean," Roper said. "It's only been a week but already . . ." He just shook his head.

"Yeah," Embry said, and laughed.

Two more men entered the room, and pretty soon the group had broken into three different conversations. As more arrived, the room got noisy, until Mrs. Varney appeared in the doorway.

"Gents, dinner is served."

They filed into the dining room in an orderly fashion, sat in the same places they usually sat in every morning and evening. There was more food involved in dinner than breakfast, and Mrs. Varney needed help bringing it all out. When she came out carrying plates, right behind her was the girl who usually stayed in the kitchen. Roper had not even met her yet. Now that he had a longer look, he could see how truly pretty she was. When she came by him and leaned over to set some plates down, he smelled her soap and a faint whiff of her sweat. Up close he could see she was closer to twenty-five than the nineteen or twenty he'd taken her for originally.

"What's your name?" he asked her.

She looked down at him as if surprised he'd spoken to her.

"Uh, Lauren," she said with a shy smile. "My name's Lauren."

He smiled, but before he could say anything else, she turned and hurried back to the kitchen.

Roper turned his attention to the fried chicken—the best he'd had in a long time.

For dessert Mrs. Varney and Lauren brought out two apple pies, sliced them up, and passed out hunks to the boarders, followed by strong black coffee. Lauren was the one who walked around the table and filled the cups. Several men spoke to her, but she didn't react. When she reached Roper, he said, "That was the best fried chicken I ever had."

She paused, looked at him, and said, "Thank you," then went back to the kitchen.

"She likes you," Catlin said.

"How can you tell?"

"Because she never talks to any of us," the lawyer said. "Never."

"Does she live in the house?" Roper asked.

"No," Catlin said, "she's got her own room somewhere else. She comes in early and leaves late."

"She goes home alone after dark?" Roper asked. "By herself?"

"Apparently," Catlin said. "She was born around here. Nobody touches her."

"She's immune to Hell's Half Acre?"

"I think she just belongs here," Catlin said.

After dinner some of the men went back to the sitting room. Others went to their own rooms. Still others went out.

Roper went to the sitting room, found Embry there with another man, talking.

"Blake," Embry said, "this is Paul Rickman. Paul also works in the yards."

Rickman looked at Roper and nodded. He was tall and rangy, probably not yet thirty. He didn't look like he was built for the tough work.

"Paul's a wrangler," Embry said. "He's got magic hands, can make a horse or a steer do whatever he wants."

"It's a gift," Rickman said.

"How long have you fellas worked in the stockyards?" Roper asked.

"I've been there a month," Embry said.

"Two months for me," Paul Rickman said. "Guess that's why we haven't found a more permanent place to live."

"There's nothin' wrong with this place," Embry said. "Can't beat the food."

"That's true," Roper said.

"We're gonna go out for a beer," Embry said. "Wanna tag along?"

"Why not?" Roper said.

33

Luckily, Embry and Rickman didn't want to go to the Bulls-head. On the other hand, they proposed going to the White Elephant, located at 106 East Exchange Avenue and the 300 block of Main Street, about as far removed—qualitywise—as you could be from Hell's Half Acre, even though it was only a matter of blocks.

"That's a pretty expensive place," Roper said.

"Don't worry about it," Rickman said. "We'll get the first two rounds."

Roper agreed to go. The White Elephant was the glittering jewel of the Fort Worth saloons and gambling halls. Brothers Bill and John Ward were the third owners of the property, and under their ownership the White Elephant offered the very best in whiskey, beer, and gambling. Cigar smoke was hanging from the high ceilings in a dark cloud, a result of the cigar shop that was situated just inside the batwing doors.

The White Elephant was certainly the type of place Talbot Roper would frequent, but for "Andy Blake" it was pricey.

Why, then, he wondered, was it not pricey for his new friends, Embry and Rickman?

They led him to the long bar, where they waved down a bartender who seemed to know who they were. So, clearly patronizing the White Elephant was not something new to them.

After they each had a cold beer in their hands, Rickman said, "I'm gonna look over the tables," and wandered off.

"Is he much of a gambler?" Roper asked.

"He likes it some," Embry said. "Me, I like to hold on to my hard-earned money."

"You know each other long?"

"Only since we met at the rooming house," Embry said. "We hit the saloons together once in a while, but we ain't what you'd call close friends."

A beautiful girl went by, carrying a tray of drinks, and Roper could see that all of the girls were lovely, and fairly young.

"A lot different than the Bullshead, huh?" he asked.

Embry wrinkled his nose and said, "The Bullshead smells bad. Even the cigar smoke here smells better than that place."

"Lots of difference in price, though."

"If you manage your money well," Embry said, "you can pretty much get what you want."

Roper had been wondering about the finances of these two men, but it was true that if you watched what you spent, and managed your money, you could pretty much do or buy what you wanted. And Embry didn't sound like a man who was earning extra money outside his job—say, for sabotage—and then spending it freely.

Maybe Embry and Rickman were not such good suspects. If it turned out they were involved in the sabotage, it would be quite a coincidence that he had ended up staying in the same rooming house with them. And Roper—like his friend Clint Adams—hated coincidence.

Rickman had secured himself a space at a roulette table, and Embry drifted over to see how he was doing. Roper remained at the bar, taking in all the White Elephant had to offer.

The place had a kitchen that catered to customers who were interested in light fare. It did not serve full dinners. It also offered separate seating for those who didn't want to eat, but only drink.

Before long, Embry and Rickman had disappeared. Roper figured they had probably gone upstairs, where there was a full casino. He decided to go up and see if they were there, and buy his round of drinks.

Upstairs was quite different from downstairs. It looked as if it had been designed by a completely different hand. The public area was decorated with fancy rosewood and mahogany fixtures shipped in from the East, thick carpets on the floor, and heavy drapes over the windows.

Every form of gambling was available and he found Embry watching Rickman at one of the roulette tables. He snagged a passing waitress and had her bring them three beers. He sipped his, alternating between looking around and watching the wheel, when he saw a familiar face across the room.

"I'll be right back," he told Embry, who simply waved that he had heard him, but kept his eyes on the table.

He walked across the room to the faro table, where a line of men were waiting to test their mettle against an expert, a man Roper had known for some time. He needed to make his presence known so that the man did not approach him, calling him by his real name.

He stood there and waited to catch the eye of famed gambler Luke Short.

34

Roper waited patiently for the dapper little gambler to look up and catch sight of him. When he did, he had to give the man credit. Roper saw only a flicker of recognition on the man's face, and that was only because he was looking for it.

Short finished what he was doing, collected the money from the players, and then signaled someone to come and replace him. The players complained, but Short calmed them down.

"Take it easy, boys," Short said. "I'll be back in a jiffy."

Short came around the table, wearing his trademark black suit, but carrying his silk top hat.

He stopped in front of Roper and said, "Damn."

"Hello, Luke."

"Who are you supposed to be?" the gambler murmured so no one else could overhear.

"Andy Blake," Roper said. "I work at the stockyards."

"Ah, I get it," Short said. "Come with me."

"You go first," Blake said. "I don't want it to look like we're friends."

"There's a private room behind a curtain in the back," Short said. "See you there."

Roper watched the little gambler disappear into the

crowd, heading for the back. He looked around to see if anyone was watching him, saw Rickman and Embry's attention still riveted to the roulette wheel. Satisfied that no one was paying him any attention, he strolled to the back, slipping between people without spilling his beer.

He found the curtain in the back and passed through it. Luke Short was waiting for him, holding a drink in his left hand, and his right hand out.

The men shook hands and Roper said, "Good to see you, Luke."

"You, too, Ro—I mean, Blake," Short said. "Working at the yards, huh? So I guess what brings you to the Fort is the trouble the cattlemen have been havin', huh?"

"Exactly."

"And undercover, I assume."

"I was even more undercover, but when I went for a job at the stockyards, I ended up being hired as a clerk."

Short started laughing, and in between bouts of laughter he said, "You . . . a . . . clerk?"

"Don't laugh," Roper said. "It puts me in a good position to learn what I need to find out."

"Who's your client?" Short asked.

"I'm working through the Pinkerton Agency," Roper said.

"You went back to the Pinkertons?"

"Just for this case," Roper said. "I went to Old Allan's funeral and his sons approached me."

"And you said yes?"

Roper shrugged.

"I'm making them pay."

"So what are you doin' here?"

"Two of my coworkers wanted to come here," Roper said. "I didn't want to make them suspicious by objecting. But I've been doing most of my drinking and eating in Hell's Half Acre."

"Any problems?"

"A few." Roper told Short what had happened so far. The gambler listened intently until he was done.

"Sounds like not everybody accepts you as a stockyard worker," he said. "I always said you had too much class."

"I guess I'll have to take some lessons when this is over," Roper said. "Get myself some rough edges."

"It's hard enough shavin' rough edges off," Short said. "Just let me know if you need any help."

"If things go right," Roper said, "you won't even be seeing me again."

"No, no," Short said, "when you finish your case, you and I are havin' a good dinner together."

"How long have you had a game here?"

"A few months," Short said, "but it's not only faro. I own the rights to all the gambling here, which makes me a one-third owner of the White Elephant."

"I'm impressed," Roper said. "Congratulations. How's the law feel about having you in business in Fort Worth?"

"We're workin' on that," Short said. "Look, I've got to get back to the table. I'm serious, Roper. If you need help, you only have to ask."

"I know that, Luke," Roper said, "and I appreciate it."

"I'll go out first," Short said. "Oh, here." He handed Roper a good cigar. "Handmade on the premises."

"Thanks. I'll follow in a few minutes," Roper said.

They shook hands again and the gambler went back through the curtain. Roper waited a few minutes, then peered out past the curtain to make sure nobody would see him come out.

Once he was back on the casino floor, he went looking for his new friends, and found them right where he'd left them.

35

Roper waited and watched with Embry until Rickman was done with the roulette wheel.

"Ya win some, ya lose some," Rickman said as he joined them. "You guys ready to go?"

"Ready," Embry said.

They walked back to Mrs. Varney's rooming house in the Half Acre.

"You guys go ahead in," Roper said. "I'm going to smoke this before I turn in."

He took the cigar out of his pocket.

"Where'd ya get that?" Embry asked.

"The White Elephant," Roper said. "Seems they're made on the premises."

"Well," Rickman said, "enjoy it. I'm goin' to bed."

"Me, too," Embry said. "Night, Blake. See ya at work tomorrow."

Roper bade both men good night and lit up his cigar. It was, indeed, a good one. He had it going to his satisfaction when the front door of the house opened and a figure stepped out. Roper turned to see who it was. As the figure came down the steps, he saw that it was the young cook, Lauren.

"Hello," he said.

"Oh," she said, surprised to find him there. "Hello."

"Are you just leaving now?" he asked, realizing it was an inane question. Obviously, she was leaving.

"Yes," she said, "I had to clean the kitchen and get it set up for breakfast in the morning."

"And you intend to walk home alone?" he asked. "At this time of night?"

"It's all right," she said. "I'll be perfectly safe."

"That's what I've heard," he said, "that you can walk through Hell's Half Acre without fear. Is that true?"

"Yes." She pulled her shawl more tightly around her shoulders.

"Why is that?"

She shrugged and said, "This is my home."

"Lots of people live here," he said. "Are they all safe?"

"I don't know about a lot of people," she said. "They might live here, but it's my home. There's a difference."

"So then you don't need me to be a gentleman and walk you home?"

"I don't."

"And if I asked you to let me, what would you say?" he asked.

"I'd say no."

"Why?"

"Because if I let you walk me home," she said, "I won't be safe anymore."

Roper drew on his cigar, let a stream of smoke go, and then nodded.

"You know," he said, "I think I understand that."

"Thank you, Mr. Blake. Good night."

"See you at breakfast," he said.

"Yes," she said, and started off down the street.

Roper continued to smoke his cigar, watching Lauren until she faded into the darkness. He wondered what it truly was about her that made her so safe in Hell's Half Acre. As far as he knew, she was just a young cook, but maybe she was much more than that.

He smoked enough of the cigar to give it the proper respect, then tossed the remainder of it into the dirt and went inside to turn in.

36

The next morning Lauren served breakfast without ever once looking at Roper. He took the hint from her and didn't try to speak.

Embry sat at one end of the table, Rickman at the other. There was still no conversation going on at the table while they all ate. Except for Roper and Catlin.

"Makin' friends?" Catlin asked.

"I've met some fellas at work," Roper said.

"What about these two?" Catlin asked. "Rickman and Embry?"

"Not friends, exactly," Roper said. "Went out with them to the White Elephant last night."

"That's an expensive place."

"Not my idea," Roper said. "I won't be goin' back. I gotta save my money."

Catlin nodded, speared another ham steak from the center of the table.

"What about you?" Roper asked. "Got friends in town?"

"Some acquaintances," the lawyer said. "No friends."

"What are you doin' stayin' in the Half Acre?" Roper said. "Doesn't seem like the place a lawyer would stay."

"This place was recommended to me as having good beds and better food. So far, I find that's the case."

"I agree."

"And I can afford it," Catlin said. "Once my practice gets up and running, I might be able to move to a nicer location. But I don't know if I'll get food this good."

"Agreed again."

"What about you?"

"Me? I don't have a career, like you. I just drift from job to job. Right now I'm a clerk at the stockyards. Not the best of jobs, but I don't have to wade through manure."

"So," Catlin said, "we're both waiting for something better."

"I guess that's true."

Roper looked around the table, saw a man—big, sloppy, beefy, mean looking—glaring at him.

"Who's that?"

"That?" Catlin asked. "That's Oscar. You know that peddler I told you about?"

"Yeah."

"He's the one we all figure gave the peddler his beating and tore up his wares."

"Underwear."

"Yep."

"And what's he glarin' at me for?"

"Maybe because you're talking."

"I'm talkin' to you," Roper said. "You're talkin'."

"But he knows I'm a lawyer."

"What's that got to do with anythin'?"

"Well, look at him," Catlin said. "Sooner or later he knows he's going to need a lawyer."

Roper grinned and said, "You're probably right."

Roper was in his room, getting ready to go to work, when there was a knock on his door. He opened it, saw Mrs. Varney standing in the hall.

"Mr. Blake."

"Mrs. Varney," he said. "Would you like to come in?"

She stared up at him sternly. "I don't go into single men's rooms."

"I see. What can I do for you, then?"

"It's Lauren."

"What about her?"

"You have to leave her alone."

"What have I done to her?" he asked.

"I see you lookin' at her," the woman said. "With that look."

"What look?"

"You know," she said. "That . . . *man* look."

"I didn't know I was doin' that," he said. "I'm sorry."

"That's what all you men say," she replied. "You didn't mean it. Well, I aim to see no harm comes to that girl."

"Seems to me she's pretty safe," Roper said.

"As long as she doesn't leave Hell's Half Acre, she is," Mrs. Varney said.

"I wonder how many people can say that," Roper said. "That they're safer inside the Half Acre than out."

"Well, she can," Mrs. Varney said, "but I also aim to make sure she's at least as safe in my house. Do you understand me?"

"I understand, Mrs. Varney," he said. "I understand you perfectly."

"Good," Mrs. Varney said. "As long as we do not have to address this matter again, you are welcome to keep your room here."

"Thank you, Mrs. Varney."

She nodded and walked away. He closed his door.

Roper was asleep a matter of hours when there was a pounding on his door. Naked, he rushed to it and opened it, gun in hand.

"What?" he asked.

"Look out your window," the lawyer, Catlin, said.

"What?"

"Look out your damned window!"

Roper turned and padded to the window, pushed the curtain aside so he could look out. In the distance he saw a glow—a flickering glow.

"Fire?" he said.

"Yes."

"Where?"

Catlin came in and stood next to him, peering out the window.

"The stockyards, Blake," he said. "The stockyards are on fire."

"Damn it," Roper said, turning and grabbing his clothes.

37

When Roper found Orton, the man's face was covered with soot.

"What happened?" he asked.

"We don't know," Orton said. "All we know is that it was ablaze. Me and some of the boys started a bucket brigade, and then the fire department arrived."

Roper looked over at the flames, which were not burning as brightly or wildly as he'd expected to find.

"It's under control," Orton said, "but we can still use all hands."

"You got 'em," Roper said, removing his jacket.

They fought the fire until dawn and after. By then Roper was as covered in soot as any of them. He'd started in a bucket brigade, then grabbed an axe and followed the firemen, knocking down burning walls so the flames wouldn't spread.

Finally, Roper and all the volunteers stepped back to allow the fire brigade to finish. The air was filled with the smell of burning wood . . . and cattle.

"How many head were lost?" he asked Orton.

"We don't know yet," Orton said, surveying the scene. "You and me, we'll have to get a count. We'll also have to assess the property damage. We lost a barn, some pens . . ."

"Anybody hurt?"

"No. We got lucky. No human fatalities."

"That's a relief."

Orton looked at him. "How'd you hear about it?"

"Somebody banged on my door and told me," Roper said.

"Well, thanks for rushing over," Orton said.

"Looks like I'm not the only one."

"We had a few men on duty. Some others saw it from their homes and came running."

Roper looked around. He had worked alongside the Fixx brothers during the night, but he still had not seen either Embry or Rickman.

"You wanna go back to your room and clean up?" Orton asked.

"What are you gonna do?"

"I'm just gonna clean up in the office," Orton said. "There's a lot to do."

"I'll come along," Roper said. "No sense going home until I can stay there and have a bath."

Orton slapped Roper on the back and said, "I was hoping you'd say that."

Once they had gone to the office and cleaned up in Orton's water closet, it was full daylight, and regular work hours. Roper and Orton came out and found most of the men standing around, looking dazed.

"What are you men doing?" Orton asked.

They looked up at him, standing on the top step in front of his office.

"We don't rightly know what to do, boss," one of them said.

"We come to work and find it's all burned up," another complained.

"It's not all burned up, you damned fools," Orton said. "Now all you fellas have to do is get back to work."

"Some of our work done burned up," another man said.

"There's a barn and some pens to be rebuilt, there are dead cattle to dispose of," Orton said. "If you don't know what you're supposed to be doing, you ask me, or ask Blake here. One of us will tell you. Now get to work!"

The men began to disperse, and Orton looked over at Roper.

"You okay with that?"

"I'm okay with it, Pete," Roper said.

"Good," he said, "now let's get to work."

Halfway through the day the local law arrived and went looking for Orton. They found Roper.

"What's your name?" one of them asked.

"Andy Blake."

"What do you do around here?"

"I'm Mr. Orton's assistant."

"Well, where is he?"

"He's around here somewhere," Roper said. "Fire last night left us with a heap of work to do."

"That's what we're here about," one of the two men said. "We're detectives with the Fort Worth Police Department."

"Why don't you wait in the office," Roper suggested, "and I'll find Mr. Orton and bring him over."

"That's right cooperative of you," the other one said. Both were dressed in suits, sporting mustaches and—Roper could tell—wearing guns under their arms. They seemed to be in their forties and were probably experienced lawmen.

"Much obliged," the other one said.

"What should I tell him your names are?"

"Carradine and Cole."

The two men walked off toward the office and Roper went in search of Orton. He found him near a corral that was being used to pile the dead beeves.

"Pete?"

"Yeah?"

"Two policemen are lookin' for you," he said. "They're at the office."

Orton turned to the other men. "Keep working." He turned to Roper. "Let's go."

"Me, too?"

"You, too."

They started walking to the office.

"Looks like this fire was arson," Orton said. "You can smell the kerosene."

"Arson," Roper said. "Who'd do that?"

"The same people who've been killing cows and causing damage for the past few months," Orton said. "Only now they're escalating to arson."

"Say," Roper said, "what about that fella that died last month. Could that have been . . ."

"Murder?" Orton asked. "I guess maybe we should leave that to the police."

38

When Orton and Roper entered the office, one of the detectives was standing by Roper's desk, the other by Orton's. They both straightened up and it was obvious they were snooping.

"Gentlemen," Orton said, "I'm Pete Orton. I understand you're looking for me?"

"That's right," the one behind Orton's desk said. "I'm Detective Carradine. This is my partner, Detective Cole."

Roper had dealt with enough law enforcement to know they didn't always work in twos. He was curious about this pair.

"Do you mind?" Orton asked, walking around his desk.

"Not at all," Carradine said, vacating the area. "Sorry."

"What can I do for you?" Orton asked.

"Actually, it's what we can do for you," Carradine said. "We're investigating the fire last night."

"Shouldn't you have been here during the fire to do that?" Roper asked.

Both detectives looked at him, then returned their attention to Orton without replying.

"Mr. Blake makes a valid point," Orton said, not letting it go.

"Unfortunately," Carradine said, "we weren't on duty at the time. But we're here now."

"And what would you like to do?"

"We'd like to see the areas that were on fire," Carradine said. "And we'd like to talk to anyone who was here last night."

"I had three men here during the night."

"Is that normal?" Carradine said. "Having men here overnight?"

"It has been since we've had all the sabotage."

"I understand you've had some accidents," Carradine said.

"Not accidents," Orton said.

"All right," Carradine said, "incidents, then."

Orton let it go. He knew they weren't accidents or incidents.

"Are you investigating those, too?" Roper asked.

The two detectives looked at him again, and this time Carradine said, "Not really, no."

"A man died," Roper said.

"That was handled by a colleague of ours," Carradine said, "and he found it to be an accident."

"Does he talk?" Roper asked, pointing at Cole.

"When he has something to say," Carradine said.

Cole ignored Roper.

"Where were you last night, sir," Carradine asked Orton, "when the fire started?"

"I was at home."

"And where's that?"

"I have a house a few miles away."

"Outside of Hell's Half Acre?"

"Yes."

"Was somebody there with you?"

"My wife."

"Okay if we talk to her at some point?" the detective asked.

"If you like."

"And how did you hear about the fire?"

"One of the men ran to my house to tell me."

Carradine turned to Roper.

"And you, sir?" he said. "Where were you?"

"Home."

"And where's that?"

"A rooming house some blocks away."

"And how did you find out about the fire?"

"One of the other boarders saw the fire from his window and woke me up."

"And what did you do?"

"I came running to see if I could help."

"And who was the boarder?"

"His name's Catlin," Roper said. "He's a lawyer."

"You think you need a lawyer, Mr. Blake?" Cole asked, speaking for the first time.

Roper looked at him in surprise.

"No," he said, "he just happens to be another boarder."

"A lawyer?" Carradine asked. "Staying in a boarding-house in the Half Acre?"

"He's new to town, has a new practice," Roper said. "When he gets it goin', he'll find someplace else to live."

"And the same for you?" Carradine asked.

"Oh yeah," Roper said. "I'm waitin' for my career here to advance."

"Advance, huh?" Carradine repeated.

Roper just stared at him. The detectives turned back to Orton.

"You got someone who can show us around?"

"Sure, Andy here can do that." Orton looked at Roper. "Okay, Andy?"

"Sure, Pete."

"I'll have the other three men waiting here when you get back," Orton said.

"Very cooperative of you," Carradine said. "Very cooperative of both of you."

"Always willing to cooperate with the law," Orton said.

"Especially since you'll be trying to find out who set the fires . . . right?"

"That's right," Carradine said, "that's what we're here for."

"I'm sure my bosses," Orton said, "will talk to your boss and extend their thanks."

"I'm sure that'll happen," Carradine said. "My boss talking to yours." He turned to Roper. "You ready, Mr. Blake? Or can I call you Andy?"

"You can call me whatever you like," Roper said. "And yeah, I'm ready."

"We'll be back soon, Mr. Orton," Carradine said. "Please have those men here."

"I said I would."

"Yes," Carradine said, "yes, you did."

39

Roper took the two police detectives around to examine the areas of the fires. The two of them walked around with their hands in their pockets, only occasionally bending over to get a better look, or maybe a whiff. In the end they both turned to Roper.

"Were there any fatalities?" Carradine asked.

"Not human," Roper said. "Just cows."

"A lot of roasted meat," Cole commented.

"What are you going to do with all that meat?" Carradine asked.

"I don't know," Roper said. "It's not up to me. Maybe we'll feed the poor."

"Now that'd be nice," Carradine said.

"Are we done here?" Roper asked.

"Sure," Carradine said, "you can take us back to the office now."

Roper started to lead the way but the two policeman suddenly flanked him.

"What do you know about your boss?" Carradine asked.

"Not much," Roper said. "He's my boss."

"Is he happy with his job?"

"As far as I know."

"What about his wife?"

"What about her?"

"Do you know her?"

"I met her once."

"Where?"

"Here at the office," Roper said. "She came to see her husband one day."

"And where are you from, Mr. Blake?" Carradine asked.

"Missouri originally," Roper said. "I moved west a long time ago, been travelin' around."

"Why'd you stop here?"

"I'd never been here before."

"How long do you plan to stay?"

"I don't have a plan," Roper said.

"That seems odd."

"Why?"

"You strike me as the kind of man who has a plan," Carradine said.

Another one who was seeing through his Andy Blake cover?

As they entered the office, four men turned to look at them.

"Detectives," Orton said from behind his desk, "these are my men, Rick John, Freddy Garcia, and Al Turnbull. They were all here last night."

"I want to thank you gents for coming in," Detective Carradine said. "We're just trying to find out what happened last night." He looked at Orton. "We'll need to speak to them separately."

"Use my office," Orton said, getting up from his chair. "Andy and I can go outside."

"Mr. Garcia and Mr. Turnbull?" Carradine asked. "Can you wait outside until we're ready?"

"Sure," Turnbull said.

"*Sí*," Garcia said.

They walked out of the office with Roper and Orton. All

four of them loitered out front, so Roper figured he'd take this opportunity to get some information.

"What'd you boys see last night?" he asked.

Both men looked at Orton, who simply nodded to them.

"I din' see nothin' until I saw the flames," Garcia said. "Then I yelled."

Roper looked at Turnbull.

"I saw a man," Turnbull said.

"Who?"

"Don't know," he answered. "Just a figure in the dark."

"Before or after the fire?"

"Before."

"What did you do?"

"I chased him," Turnbull said, "but then I heard Freddy yell. When I saw the fire, I wasn't sure what to do, but I thought the fire the biggest danger."

"You did the right thing," Orton said. "You fellas raised the alarm, maybe saved us a lot more damage."

Turnbull nodded. He and Garcia walked off to one side and rolled some cigarettes, leaving Orton and Roper alone.

"Did you know that?" Roper asked. "About Turnbull seein' somebody."

"He told me just before you came in with the detectives."

"So this was definitely arson."

"I figured that all along."

"But this confirms it."

"You tell your bosses yet?"

"No," Orton said. "I'm meeting with them later today. Hey, you want to come?"

Roper thought that over. He didn't know for sure who was paying Orton's salary. He thought maybe that was something he should know, even if the man's bosses had to be in on hiring the Pinkertons.

"I'd like that," Roper said.

"We'll do it right after work," Orton said. "For now I think we'll just wait here until these policemen are done."

Roper looked over at Turnbull and Garcia, who were both

smoking. After fighting the fire most of the morning, a cigarette was the last thing Roper wanted.

They waited there until the policemen questioned all three men. When Rick John came out, Roper asked him what he had seen, but he was like Garcia. He didn't see anything until after the fire started.

Once the three men had been questioned, Orton sent them home rather than back to work. They'd been awake a long time.

Orton and Roper reentered the office, found Carradine sitting at Orton's desk, and Cole seated behind Roper's.

"Did you get what you wanted?" Orton asked.

"Pretty much," Carradine said.

"Then can I get my desk and my office back?"

"By all means." Carradine stood up. Cole remained seated. In fact, he put his feet up on the desk. Roper walked over and stared down at him. Cole glared back.

"Can I ask why the sheriff isn't here asking questions?" Roper asked.

"We've taken control of this case," Carradine said. "There won't be any need for you to see the sheriff." He looked at his partner. "Come on, Cole," Carradine said. "We better get back to the station."

Cole looked over at his partner, then slowly put his feet down on the floor and stood up.

"You and me," Roper said, "we ain't gonna be buyin' each other any Christmas presents, are we?"

Cole stared at Roper and said, "There's somethin' off about you, friend. I'm gonna find out what it is."

"Just ask me, friend," Roper said. "I got nothin' to hide."

"We'll see," Cole said.

"We'll be in touch, Mr. Orton," Carradine said.

Orton just nodded as the two detectives went out the door.

"That Cole's got it in for you for some reason," Orton said.

"I know it."

"You don't have a price on your head somewhere, do you, Andy?"

"Not that I know of."

"Let's get back to work," the man said. "We still got a lot of damage to assess."

When they went back outside, the two detectives were nowhere in sight.

"You think those fellas are really gone?" Orton asked.

"They may be gone," Roper said, "but I doubt they're done."

40

At the end of the day Orton and Roper went back into the office.

"Not a good day," Orton said, shaking his head and sitting behind his desk. "I still got some paperwork to do, but why don't you go home and get cleaned up? Meet me back here in a couple of hours. We'll go see my bosses, and then get some dinner somewhere."

Roper was going to hate to miss dinner at Mrs. Varney's, but he said, "Yeah, okay. I'll see you then."

When he got back to the rooming house, Mrs. Varney was setting the table for dinner.

"I hate to bother you, ma'am, but I'd like to take a bath. Would that be possible?"

She glared at him and said, "Lauren can finish up here. I'll draw the bath for you, Mr. Blake. Will you be eating dinner with us?"

"No, ma'am," Roper said. "I got an appointment with my boss."

Looking unhappy, she went to draw his bath. Roper had learned that Mrs. Varney never looked happy.

* * *

Freshly bathed, wearing fresh clothes that didn't smell like smoke, Roper came down the stairs and ran into both Embry and Rickman.

"Where have you fellas been?" he asked.

"We both had the day off," Rickman said. "We been gamblin'."

"He's been gamblin'," Embry said. "I was watchin'. Why?"

"You didn't hear about the fire?"

"We heard somethin' about a fire," Rickman said, "but we was busy."

"It was the stockyards that were burnin'."

"Whoa," Embry said. "We still got jobs?"

"It didn't burn down, did it?" Rickman asked.

"No," Roper said, "we fought it until the brigade got there, but we sure coulda used your help."

"It was our day off," Rickman said, as if that excused everything, and the two men went in to dinner.

Roper heard somebody descending the stairs behind him, looked, and saw Catlin coming down.

"Hey, how'd you make out last night?" the lawyer asked.

"It wasn't as bad as it could've been," Roper said. "We managed to fight it off until the brigade got there. I really appreciate you wakin' me up."

"No problem."

"I'm glad I ran into you," Roper said. "We had some detectives askin' us questions about where we were last night. They might come to talk to you about wakin' me up."

"Don't worry," Catlin said, "I'll tell them you were in bed until I woke you."

"Thanks."

"And if you need a lawyer for any reason," the man went on, "let me know. I'll give you a good friend discount."

"I appreciate that."

The two men shook hands and split up, Catlin to go to dinner, and Roper to go back to the stockyards.

* * *

When he met up with Orton at the office, his boss had also cleaned up and changed his clothes.

"You look better," Orton said.

"And neither one of us smells like smoke," Roper pointed out.

"Funny," Orton said, "I can still smell it. Must be the inside of my nostrils."

Roper knew what he meant.

"Those detectives come back?" Roper asked.

"Not that I know of," Orton said. "They talk to that lawyer friend of yours?"

"Not yet. How about your wife?"

"I don't know," Orton said. "I didn't go home, I cleaned up here. Come on, turns out we're going to meet my bosses for dinner. On them. Not bad, eh?"

"Not bad. Where are we eatin'?" Roper asked.

"Someplace that's supposed to have the best steaks in town," Orton said. "The Cattleman's Club."

"The Cattleman's Club?" Roper asked.

"Yeah, I know," Orton said. "Nobody usually gets in there to eat unless they're a member, but we're going to be guests."

Roper was glad he hadn't gone in or out the front door of the Cattleman's Club the first time he was there. Nobody was liable to recognize him, except for that kitchen worker, as well as Mr. Kalish. Hopefully, neither of them would say a word.

41

When they crossed out of Hell's Half Acre, they grabbed a cab to the Cattleman's Club. A beefy doorman opened the door of the enclosed coach for them, and they stepped out.

"Are you gentlemen members?" the doorman inquired.

"No," Orton said.

"Then I'm afraid you can't go inside," the man said. He was wearing a red coat and a black top hat. "This is a private club." Roper was impressed with the width of the man's shoulders.

"I understand that," Orton said. "We're guests. We've been invited to dinner."

"By whom, sir?"

"Mr. Kalish."

Oh great, Roper thought.

"Come with me, please." The doorman led them to the front door, allowed them to step just inside. "Wait here, please."

"He's going to be surprised when they tell him to let us in," Orton said.

Roper wondered what Orton would think if he told him they were both working for the same man.

* * *

The doorman returned a few minutes later and said, "Please follow me, sirs."

He led them down a long hall, past sitting rooms Roper had seen the last time he was there.

At the end of a hall the doorman opened a door and said, "Inside, sirs. Enjoy your dinner."

"Thank you," Roper said.

They walked in, found a long table—much like Mrs. Varney's, but made of much more expensive wood, rosewood with a high shine on it—with well-dressed men sitting around it. Among them was Mr. Harold Kalish.

But Kalish wasn't sitting at the head of the table. Another man was. He was younger than Kalish, dark-haired, pale-skinned, hair perfectly cut, suit more expensive than anyone else's. The room itself had high ceilings, dark-paneled walls, and windows covered with expensive gold-bordered brocade drapes of green and maroon.

"Welcome, Mr. Orton. Who is that you've got with you?" the man asked.

"Good evening, Mr. Brewster," Orton said. "This is my assistant, Andy Blake."

Roper looked at Kalish, who—to his credit—was making every effort not to meet his eyes. Perhaps he thought he wouldn't be able to keep their secret if he did.

"Welcome, Mr. Blake," Brewster said. "I'm Cullen Brewster. And starting on my right and going around the table are Mr. Harold Kalish, Mr. Adrian Arnold, Mr. Edward Halfwell, and Mr. George Mannerly."

Halfwell and Mannerly looked to be in their eighties and barely conscious of what was going on around them. Arnold was Kalish's age, while Brewster seemed to be the youngest of them. This had to be the brain trust of the cattle interests in Fort Worth, the men who hired the Pinkertons. And Kalish was simply his contact.

"Have a seat, gentlemen," Brewster said, "and we'll start dinner."

There was a chair at the end of the table, on each side. Roper hesitated while Orton walked to the table and sat next to Kalish. Roper sat across from him, next to Edward Halfwell, who smelled vaguely of something . . . old.

As if by some signal, the doors opened and several waiters entered carrying trays. The room suddenly filled with delicious smells. They all sat back while the waiters served them. Kalish continued to avoid Roper's eyes, which was fine with the detective.

Before long, they had plates full of food in front of them, one of which held a stack of steaks.

"Dig in, gents," Brewster said.

Each man speared a steak with a fork and passed the plate on. Then they did the same with potatoes, onions, and carrots.

The waiters reentered and placed a cold mug of beer next to each man. After that a glass, which they filled with red wine. Each man had his choice to drink one or the other, or both.

Lastly, a glass of water was set before them all, and then a man—the head waiter—said to Brewster, "Will there be anything else, sir?"

"No, that'll be all, Henry," Brewster said. "I'll ring if we need anything."

"Yes, sir."

The head waiter withdrew and the men began to eat.

"Mr. Orton—Pete . . ." Brewster said, "perhaps while we eat, you can fill us in on what happened last night."

"Of course," Orton said, and began talking.

Roper concentrated on his dinner and allowed Orton to fill the gentlemen in.

Orton managed to talk and devour half his steak at the same time. The other men ate and listened, with only Brewster asking an occasional question.

Roper was surprised to see the two older men eating the steak, albeit after cutting it into small pieces. They may not have been in possession of all their faculties—or maybe they were—but he was sure they had the money to be part of this group.

"What about the police?" Brewster asked after Orton was done.

"They came this morning, two detectives from the Fort Worth Police Department. They asked questions, but I don't know . . , I don't know if they care to find out who did it."

Roper looked around the table. Kalish kept his eyes averted. He wondered how many men seated at that table knew who he really was. It was only supposed to be Kalish, but Brewster seemed to be the man in charge. Had Kalish shared the information with him?

"Well," Brewster said, "we've taken steps to ensure that we find out who's doing it."

"Really?" Orton asked. "Like what?"

Just at that moment Kalish looked at Roper and flushed. He looked like a guilty man about to be exposed. If Orton had been looking at him, he certainly would have caught on that something was wrong. But luckily, Orton was looking at Brewster.

"It's not necessary that you know that," Brewster said. "Just rest assured it's being taken care of."

"So what do you want me to do?" Orton asked.

"Business as usual," Brewster said.

"We're going to need money and supplies to rebuild the structures that burned down. And we need to do something with the cows that were killed."

"How many head did you lose?" Adrian Arnold asked.

"About twenty."

"Not too bad," Kalish said.

"Could've been worse," Brewster agreed. "And we want you to know we've had a meeting about you and we're giving you a vote of confidence. We know none of this is your fault."

"Thank you," Orton said.

"Yes," Arnold said, "your job is secure."

Orton nodded, pushed his plate away. "I'm happy to hear that."

"You don't say much, do you, Mr. Blake?" Brewster commented.

Roper had finished his steak and had just been listening.

"Not my place, Mr. Brewster," he said. "Mr. Orton's the boss. I'm just the assistant."

"But what do you think of all this?"

"Seems to me if you've taken steps to make sure these people are identified, caught, and punished, you should all just sit back and wait."

He knew his words had special meaning to Kalish. He didn't know if any of the others knew, or cared.

"Seems to me you're right," Brewster said, "but I'm thinking this better come to an end soon, or we're going to lose some big Eastern investors."

"Business always comes down to the investors," Roper said.

"Andy!" Orton said sharply.

"No, no, Pete," Brewster said. "I asked him what he thought. Yes, Mr. Blake, business does always come down to the money." He looked at Orton. "Speaking of which, I'll have some cash brought by your office tomorrow morning."

"Good," Orton said. "Thank you."

Brewster smiled and said, "Now let's have some coffee."

After coffee, Roper felt that he and Orton were dismissed. Orton thanked his bosses for dinner, and they were shown out of the building.

"I don't know if it was so smart, talking to the bosses like that," Orton said outside.

"Hey," Blake said, "they asked me."

"Yeah, well . . ."

"Sorry if I embarrassed you."

"You didn't," Orton said.

"Good. You better head home," Roper said. "Your wife is probably wondering where the hell you are."

"If she's home," Orton said. "Lately, I don't know where the hell she goes."

"You mean, if she's not coming by the office asking for money?"

"Yeah," Orton said, "right. Look, I'll see you in the morning. I'll try to get in before the money man shows up, so you won't have the responsibility."

"I'd put the money in the safe, but I don't know the combination . . ." Roper said, then quickly added, "and I don't want to."

"Well," Orton said, "if you stay on long enough, that may change. I'll see you in the morning."

"Night," Roper said.

He watched Orton walk away. The man made no move to find a cab, and Roper suddenly doubted he was actually going back home.

He decided to follow him.

42

Orton obviously had no inkling that anyone would want to follow him. He never looked behind him as he strode purposefully down the street.

Just to be safe, however, Roper tailed him with care, keeping to the darkened side of the street.

Orton led the way to a neighborhood that was halfway between Hell's Half Acre and the Cattleman's Club. Finally, he turned down a side street, and soon they were walking with small homes on either side of them.

Orton finally reached his destination, a small, A-frame house with a white fence in front of it. He opened the gate and walked to the front door, where he knocked. Roper rushed to get into position but the door closed again before he could see who was inside.

He waited a few moments for the people inside the house to get settled, then crossed the street. He went through the same gate, then around to one side of the house. He found a window and peered in, saw no one. He moved on to another window, but had to go to a third before he saw two people in a clinch. As he watched, they kissed each other, their hands roaming all over. They were in a bedroom, and before long the clothes started coming off and then they were on the bed.

So Pete Orton was cheating on his wife. So what? That had nothing to do with sabotage, did it?

As he watched, they began to make love. Roper had watched many people do many things over the years, including having sex. It didn't faze him. He wasn't particularly interested in it—not as an activity anyway. No, what he wanted to see was who the woman was. He still had not been able to get a look at her face.

On the bed Orton was on top of the woman, and her face was turned away from the window. Roper waited, but she never turned his way. They continued their amorous activity, and before long rolled over so that the woman was on top, straddling him. She had beautiful skin, excellent breasts, and long hair, and as she rode him, she tossed her head back, then shook it from side to side. Finally she stopped long enough for Roper to see her face. He knew her. Here was a perfect example of the coincidences Roper hated so much.

The woman was Nancy Ransom.

Roper waited across the street.

He didn't know whose house they were in, Orton had his own home with his wife, while Nancy had a room above the Bullshead Saloon. That meant this house had to belong to someone else, and finding out who that was might shed some light on things.

So he waited, and eventually, two hours later, Orton left the house. Roper watched him walk away until he was out of sight, then settled back to wait some more. He was on the porch of a house that seemed to be vacant, and he was in the shadows so that no one could see him.

An hour later Nancy Ransom opened the front door and stepped out. She looked around, as if making sure no one could see her, then closed the door and walked to the gate. She looked again, and at one moment she stared across the street and Roper wondered if she knew she was looking right at him.

Finally, she opened the gate, stepped out, closed it behind her, and walked down the street in the same direction Orton had gone. He gave her time to fade from sight, then left his perch and crossed the street again. The neighborhood had seemed quiet when they arrived, and Roper now knew it was because many of the homes were vacant.

To be on the safe side, though, he went to the rear of the house and found the back door.

He let himself in.

Back at the Cattleman's Club, after Roper and Orton left, the other men shared an after-dinner brandy before three of them—Arnold and the two older gentlemen—left the room. Brewster and Kalish remained.

"Harold," Brewster said, "don't you think it's time for you to let me in on the secret?"

"What secret is that, Cullen?"

"You know," Brewster said. "The identity of the Pinkerton agent?"

"I don't think so."

"Good God, why not?" the other man demanded.

"I told you," Kalish answered, "Pinkerton's condition was that only one person know who their operative was."

"I don't see why—"

"If anyone else became aware of his identity," Kalish went on, "I was told he would cease and desist immediately, and return to Chicago."

Angrily, Brewster stood up and pointed at Kalish.

"This had better work," he said. "If we incur any more damage or expense, I'm holding you personally responsible."

As Brewster left the room, leaving Kalish alone, the man took out a cigar and lit it. The only thing that ever calmed him down when he was agitated was a good cigar.

This one, he thought, had better be real good.

43

Roper went through the house methodically.

As he entered through the back door, he found himself in the kitchen, so he decided to start there. There was nothing there to indicate who owned the house, or that it was even occupied.

He moved on to the house's living and dining rooms. The search there was easy, as there was no furniture in either room.

The house was very small, and had only one bedroom. Roper went in there and found that the only furniture was the bed. No tables or chest of drawers, no clothing in the closet. This house was obviously meant for just one thing, and that was as a place for Orton and Nancy to have their clandestine meetings.

But somebody owned it. Somebody had to.

Roper went through the house one last time to satisfy himself that he hadn't missed anything. Then he went back out the rear door.

When he got back to the rooming house, nobody was around, and the downstairs was dark. He went up to his room, passed a couple of doors showing light beneath them.

He didn't know who they belonged to, and didn't give it much thought.

In his room he got ready for bed, reflecting on the events of the day. Could Pete Orton's infidelity be connected in some way to the acts of sabotage? He thought maybe finding out who owned the house they were using might be helpful.

He went to sleep on that thought.

Early the following morning a man left the Cattleman's Club carrying a package. The doorman got him a cab. He settled back in his seat while the driver waved the reins at the horse.

The man watched the streets go by until he realized they weren't heading for the stockyards.

"Hey, driver?" he called.

No reply.

"Driver!"

The cab was an open one, so he could see the back of the driver, but the man didn't seem to be hearing him.

He leaned forward and started to reach to tap the man on the shoulder. At that point the man turned, pointed a gun at the messenger, and shot him through the heart. As his victim slumped to the floor of the cab, the driver returned his attention to his driving.

Ten minutes later the cab pulled to a stop before a vacant lot between two vacant buildings. Right across the street was the line of demarcation to Hell's Half Acre.

The driver got down and rolled the body of the messenger out of the cab and into the lot, then bent over and retrieved the package he was delivering from his pocket. He looked inside, found that it was filled with cash, as expected. He smiled, because this was his payment for a job well done.

When Roper got to work that day, Orton was already there and already agitated.

"What's goin' on?" Roper asked.

"I'm waiting for the messenger to come with the money Brewster promised us," Orton said. "He was supposed to be here early."

"You thinkin' Brewster changed his mind?"

"He better not have."

"Maybe somethin' happened to the messenger."

"Yeah, maybe . . ."

"Why don't I go and find out?" Roper suggested.

"How?"

"I'll go to the Cattleman's Club and see Brewster. Find out if and when the messenger left. If he did, then maybe I can find out what happened to him. It's better than just sittin' here waitin'."

"Yeah, you're right about that," Orton said. "I'd go myself, but I've got a hell of a lot of work here because of the fire."

"That's okay," Roper said, "I can take care of it."

"Yeah, okay," Orton said, "you do that. But hey—"

"Yeah?"

"Watch your back," Orton said, "just in case something did happen to the messenger."

"Okay, sure," Roper said.

"You're not wearing a gun," Orton said. "Here." He opened a drawer and brought out a .32 Colt. "Stick this in your belt."

Roper crossed the room, accepted the gun, and tucked it into his belt. "Thanks."

44

Roper had been trying to think all morning of a way to get away from the stockyards. He wanted to go and check on the ownership of the house he had followed Orton to. In order to do that, he needed to check on the deed. That meant a trip to the county clerk's office. But before that, he needed to check on the messenger.

He went directly to the Cattleman's Club and presented himself at the front door.

"My name's Andy Blake," he said. "Pete Orton sent me over to talk to Mr. Brewster."

"Please wait here," the doorman said.

Roper waited. The man returned moments later and said, "Follow me, sir."

Roper followed the doorman to an office, which he found odd. Was it possible that Brewster actually ran the Cattleman's Club and was not just a member?

Brewster was behind the desk as he entered and stood up. The office was expensively furnished, with wood and gold-plated surfaces gleaming. Brewster was once again wearing an expensive three-piece suit, this one charcoal gray, and his hair had so much pomade in it that it gleamed, almost outshining the other surfaces. And the scent he was wearing almost made Roper's eyes water.

"Mr. Blake, isn't it?"

"That's right," Roper said as the doorman withdrew. "Pete Orton sent me to check and see if you were sending the money you promised over by messenger."

"I don't understand," Brewster said. "The messenger left here early this morning." ·

"He never arrived," Roper said. "Was he trustworthy?"

"Very trustworthy," Brewster said. "I have used him before for larger sums of money. If he was going to steal from me, it would not be this particular package."

"Then somethin' must've happened to him," Roper said.

"Excuse me," Brewster said, coming around the desk. "I want to get the doorman back in here."

He was gone a few minutes and returned with the man who had shown Roper in.

"This is Lester," Brewster said to Roper. "Lester, tell Mr. Blake what you told me."

"The messenger left here at seven thirty this morning," Lester said.

"Left how?" Roper asked.

"Sir?"

"Was he walking? Riding?"

"Oh, I see," Lester said. "No, sir, I got him a cab."

"Did you know the driver?"

"Now that you mention it, no, sir."

"Do you usually know the drivers?"

"Yes, sir," Lester said, "usually."

"Could it be he was just a new driver?"

"New drivers usually introduce themselves," Lester said.

"And this one didn't."

"No, sir."

"What direction did the cab go when it left?" Roper asked.

"It pulled away and went down the street," the doorman said.

"Did you see if it turned when it reached the corner," Roper asked, "or continued on?"

"No, sir," the doorman said. "I didn't notice."

Roper looked at Brewster.

"All right, Lester," the man said. "Thank you. You can go back to the door."

"Yes, sir.

Brewster sat down.

"Do you think something happened to my man?" he asked Roper.

"If he didn't steal the money," Roper said, "then yes. What's his name?"

"Mark Vaughn," Brewster said. "This is his business, making deliveries. And sometimes those deliveries include lots of money."

"And you trust him."

"Implicitly."

"Then something must have happened."

Brewster put his head in his hands.

"More sabotage," he said.

"I'm going to look for him," Roper said.

"I should call for the police," Brewster said.

"Yes, you probably should."

The man raised his head and looked at Roper, who suddenly realized he'd been acting like himself, and not like Andy Blake.

"Why did Orton send you over here?" he asked.

"He has a lot of work because of the fire," Roper said. "I offered to come over and check on the messenger."

Brewster studied him for a moment, then said, "Who are you?"

Roper had a decision to make. He could reveal himself to Brewster, who was, after all, one of the people paying the Pinkertons for his services. Or he could remain Andy Blake, maintain his cover, which would be the professional thing to do.

Roper always went by his instinct, though. If his instinct

was telling him to step out from behind the mask, he would. But it wasn't doing that. Not yet.

"I'm just Andy Blake, Mr. Brewster," he said. "I'm just tryin' to do my job."

"Seems to me you're going a little beyond your job, Andy," Brewster said, "and I appreciate it. I'll send for the police while you get started. Maybe you can find Mark before the police need to act."

"Maybe I can," Roper said. "I'll let you know, sir."

"Can I walk you out?" Brewster offered.

"No need, sir," Roper said, "I can find my way back out. I might have another word with the doorman on the way."

"Yes, of course," Brewster said. "Lester is at your disposal."

"Thank you, Mr. Brewster."

"Andy?" Brewster called as Roper started out the door.

"Sir?"

"Do you need any money? I mean, for expenses?"

"No, sir," Roper said, "I'm fine. Thanks."

"No," Brewster said, "thank *you*, Andy."

45

Roper left the Cattleman's Club with an odd feeling about Cullen Brewster. There was definitely something too . . . obsequious . . . about him. Especially that last "No, thank *you*, Andy." During their meal the previous evening there had been no inkling of that side of the man. In fact, he had come across rather cold and stern.

No, the man had been putting on an act, but why?

Roper stopped outside the door to speak to Lester.

"Sir?"

"I wonder if you can talk to some of the cab drivers you know, see if any of them knows the man who picked up Mr. Vaughn."

"I can do that, sir."

"Thank you."

"If it's all right with Mr. Brewster."

"It is," Roper said. "In fact, he's put you at my disposal. But you should ask him, just to satisfy yourself."

"Yes, sir."

"Tell me, Lester," Roper said, "does Mr. Brewster own the Cattleman's Club?"

"No, sir," Lester said, "he simply manages it."

"I see. Can you get me a cab?"

"Certainly, sir."

Roper waited while Lester waved down a cab, then got in and told the driver, "The county clerk's office."

"Yes, sir."

When they reached their destination, Roper got down but, before paying the driver, asked him some questions.

"Have you seen any strange drivers around lately?" he asked.

"Strange how?"

"New," Roper said.

"Naw," the man said. "No new drivers." He took off his hat and a shock of gray hair fell down over his forehead. Prematurely so, though, as he seemed to be in his thirties.

"Ask around, will you?" Roper asked. "If anybody has seen someone strange, have them talk to Lester, at the Cattleman's Club."

"Yes, sir."

Roper paid the fare, then handed the man an extra dollar.

"Wait for me," he said. "I won't be long, and I want you to help me find something."

"Like what, sir?"

"A good place to dump a dead body."

It didn't take long for Roper to find the information he wanted. He had a clerk look up the deed to the address of the house Orton was using for his love nest.

"Yes, sir, here it is," the clerk said. "It is owned by a Mr. Cullen Brewster."

"Brewster?"

"Yes, sir."

"Are you sure?"

The clerk looked again and said, "It's right here, sir." He showed Roper where the name was written.

"Yep," Roper said, "that says Brewster."

He had not expected the owner to be one of the men from the dinner table the night before.

"All right," Roper said, "thanks."

He turned to leave, then paused and looked back at the clerk.

"Can you tell me when Mr. Brewster bought the property?"

"Sure," the clerk said. He checked the book, then said, "Last month, actually."

"And who did he buy it from?"

The clerk lowered his head again. "A Mr. George Mannerly." The man looked up. "Oh! Isn't Brewster the man who runs—"

"Yes, he is. Thank you."

Outside, the driver was still waiting but with a worried look on his face.

"Sir," he said as Roper got into the back, "did you say . . . someplace to dump a body?"

"Yes, I did."

"But . . . do you have a body?"

"No," Roper said, "I'm looking for one. Let's say you picked up a man in front of the Cattleman's Club, but instead of taking him where he wanted to go, you decided to kill him, rob him, and dump his body. Where would you take him?"

"Well . . . I can think of a few places."

"Let's go and check them," Roper said.

"Am I gettin' paid, sir?"

"Oh yeah," Roper said, "you're gettin' paid."

"Okay, then."

The driver took Roper to a building site, thinking the body might have been dumped in the excavation. Then he took him to an empty lot. Finally, he drove to a lot between two abandoned buildings, just across from where Hell's Half Acre started.

"What do you think?" Roper asked, stepping down. "Inside one of the buildings?"

"I guess," the driver said, "or just in the lot."

Roper figured it depended on whether or not the killer wanted to hide the body or not. Apparently, he didn't, because as soon as Roper stepped into the lot, he saw the body.

Roper walked over and examined it. The man had been shot through the heart, killed with one shot.

"Well, I'll be damned," the driver said. "You some kind of a detective, or somethin'?"

Roper looked up at the driver and said, "Or somethin'."

46

Roper stayed with the body and sent the driver—whose name was Jamie—for the police. When they arrived, he was surprised to see Detectives Cole and Carradine.

"Well, well, Mr. Blake," Carradine said. "What do we have here?"

"I think it's a man named Mark Vaughn," Roper said. "He's been shot."

Carradine leaned down over the body and said, "He sure has, right through the heart." He straightened up. "What's your connection?"

"I'm just tryin' to help out, Detective."

"Help who?"

"Mr. Brewster, at the Cattleman's Club. You see, this man was a messenger for him, and was carryin' a lot of money this mornin'."

"Is that a fact? And where was he taking that money?"

"To Mr. Orton, at the stockyards."

"Orton? Your boss?"

"That's right."

"And how is it you're the one who found the body?" Cole asked.

"Like I said," Roper replied. "I'm just tryin' to help."

"Well," Carradine said, "maybe you can help us."

"How can I do that?"

"Accompany us to the police station, where we can have a nice private talk."

"I'm supposed to go back to work—"

"We'll send Mr. Orton a message," Carradine promised, "so you don't get fired."

"I really appreciate that," Roper said.

"Comin' with us, then?" Cole asked.

"Why would I not?" Roper asked.

"No reason," Carradine said. "I just think my partner was hoping you'd resist."

Roper looked at Cole and said, "Sorry to disappoint you."

They took Roper to the police station on West Belknap Street. They walked him to a small room and left him to sit by himself at a narrow table for a while. He knew they were softening him up. As Talbot Roper, this was something he was used to. But Andy Blake wouldn't be so calm.

"Hey, come on!" he shouted, banging on the locked door. "I got to get back to work!"

He heard the lock click, and the door opened. A man wearing a marshal's badge walked in. He was a large man, barrel-chested and ham-handed, with a full head of gray hair and wrinkles he'd earned over the course of about sixty years.

"Mr. Blake. My name's Marshal Ben Gates."

"Marshal," Roper said. "I was expecting the detectives."

"I'm here to take you to the detectives," the marshal said. "I think they made a mistake locking you in this room. After all, you're only here to help us, right?"

"That's right."

"Well, the detectives have been reprimanded for the way they've treated you. However, I'm going to ask you to submit to their questions, as they know what to ask and I do not."

"I understand, Marshal."

"Thank you, sir. Now, if you'll follow me?"

Marshal Gates led Roper back along the same hallway the detectives had brought him in by, but ducked into an open doorway halfway along. This time instead of being in a bare room meant for interrogation, he found himself in a small office with two little desks. They were made to look even smaller with Carradine and Cole sitting behind them.

"Mr. Blake has agreed to help," the marshal said, "even though you two have mistreated him."

"Marshal—" Cole started.

"Shut up, Cole!" Gates said. He turned to Roper. "Sir, again my thanks for your cooperation. If these two detectives give you a hard time, please let me know."

"Thank you, Marshal."

Marshal Gates left the room and Roper turned to face the two detectives. He was sure that all three law enforcement officials thought he had bought the act they'd just put on for him. Or for "Andy Blake" anyway. Talbot Roper had seen that kind of dog-and-pony show too many times before to be fooled.

Roper looked around the small room for a chair, but there wasn't one.

"Don't worry about sitting down," Cole said. "You won't be here that long."

"That sounds good to me."

"Just fill us in on your actions today, Blake," Carradine said. "Start from this morning and take us through to finding the body."

Roper gave them an account of his day, telling the truth as much as he could. He wanted it to sound like he'd pretty much stumbled over the body, rather than found it through detective footwork.

When he was finished, both detectives stared at him.

"You know we'll be checking your story with Brewster, the doorman, and the driver, right?" Carradine said.

"I do," Roper said. "You wanted the truth, though, and I gave it to you. Can I go back to work now?"

"What do you think, Cole?" Carradine asked.

"I think he knows more than he's saying," Cole answered, "but hell, let him go back to work. We know where to find him."

"Yeah, we do," Carradine said. "So go ahead, Blake. Get back to work."

"You'll let me know if the money he was carrying shows up, won't you?"

"Why would I do that?" Carradine asked. "It was Brewster who sent the money out. We find anything, we'll let him know."

"Good enough," Roper said. "Tell Marshal Gates for me you fellas were perfect gentlemen."

"Get outta here!" Cole growled.

Instead of going back to the stockyards, Roper went to see the sheriff. The man looked up at him as he entered the shoebox-sized office.

"Mr. Blake, isn't it?" Reynolds said. "What can I do for you?"

"I was just wondering," Roper said. "You said you were going to be keeping an eye on me, but I ain't seen you since. And I've been having some problems."

"So I've heard," Reyolds said.

"So then the detectives have talked to you."

"Carradine and Cole, yeah," Reynolds said. "Charming pair."

"They tell you what to do? Is that it?"

"Fort Worth is leaning heavily toward having a police department, and no sheriff," Reynolds said. "You can tell that from my new office here. So I'm tryin' to get myself as many paychecks as possible before they make me scarce. If that means lettin' the detectives investigate whatever they want, then so be it. And they seem to want you."

"I get it," Roper said.

"Maybe you do, and maybe you don't," Reynolds said. "But this town—this *city*—doesn't have much use for me, and the feeling is pretty mutual."

"Okay, then," Roper said. "Now I know."

"Now you know," Reynolds said. "Good luck to you."

47

When Roper entered the stockyard office, Orton looked up from his desk and said, "Where the hell have you been?"

"The law said they were gonna let you know," Roper told him.

"Well, they didn't," Orton said. "Let me know what?"

Roper filled him in, just the way he had told it to the police.

"Jesus Christ!" Orton exploded. "I knew Mark Vaughn. Dead, you say?"

"Shot dead."

"Have you told Brewster?"

"No," Roper said. "I came here first so you wouldn't fire me."

"Well, you're not fired," Orton said. "Get your ass over to the Cattleman's and let Brewster know what's going on."

"Yes, sir."

As Roper headed for the door, Orton said, "Hey, Andy."

"Yeah?" Roper asked at the door.

"Good work."

"Thanks."

* * *

Back at the Cattleman's Club, Lester was still on duty.

"I've spoken with several of the drivers, sir," he said. "Nobody knows anything about a strange driver."

"Okay, Lester," he said. "Thanks. Can I get in to see Mr. Brewster?"

"Yes, sir," the doorman said. "I've been instructed to take you right to him when you arrived. Follow me."

Roper followed the man's broad back into the club, but this time not to Brewster's office. They went to one of the sitting rooms, where Brewster was talking with several well-dressed gentlemen. When he spotted Lester and Roper, he excused himself and walked over.

"I hope this is important," he said to them.

"I found Mark Vaughn," Roper said. "He's been shot and killed. That important enough for you?"

"All right, Lester," Brewster said, dismissing the doorman. "Mr. Blake, can we talk over here, please?"

Brewster took Roper's arm and pulled him aside, away from prying eyes and ears.

"Tell me."

"Not much to tell," Roper said. "Looks like a phony cab driver picked him up, shot him through the heart, and dumped him in an empty lot just this side of Hell's Half Acre."

"And the money?"

"Gone."

"What about the police?"

"They're on it," Roper said. "The marshal has these two detectives, Carradine and Cole, working on it."

"Are they good men?"

Roper started to answer, then stopped himself and went another way. "How would I know?"

"I don't know," Brewster said, "but I get the feeling you would."

"I have to get back to work, Mr. Brewster," Roper said. "Mr. Orton wants to know about the money you promised."

"Well, it's gone—" Brewster started, then stopped and calmed himself. "Okay, tell him . . . tell him I'll have it replaced. I should be able to get it to him tomorrow morning."

"I'll tell him."

Roper started away, and Brewster called after him.

"And tell him to send you for it this time," the man said. "No more messengers."

"Sure," Roper said, "no more messengers."

Roper left, decided to walk most of the way back, try to get everything straight in his head. Pete Orton was having an affair with Nancy Ransom, using a house that used to be owned by Mannerly, but was now owned by Brewster, who was one of the men—apparently one of five men—who had hired the Pinkertons.

Kalish was supposed to be the only one of the five who knew who and what Roper really was. Although Brewster seemed to suspect that "Andy Blake" was something other than what he seemed to be, he had given no indication he knew the truth.

But Brewster seemed to be the head honcho, running the Cattleman's Club, spearheading the group of five who seemed in control of the cattle business in Fort Worth. He was also the man who had sent the messenger out with the money—the messenger who had then been killed. Who besides Brewster knew what Mark Vaughn had been carrying? Damn it, he should have asked that question, but he didn't want to come off too much like a detective with Brewster—not yet anyway.

But it might be getting close to the time when Talbot Roper had to come out from behind the mask.

48

When Roper got back to the office, he gave Orton the message about the money.

"You mean he's going to replace it himself?"

"I don't know how he's gonna do it, boss, but he's gonna do it," Roper said. "You should have it tomorrow, only . . ."

"Only what?"

"Well, he wants me to come and pick it up," Roper said. "Doesn't want to take the chance of another messenger, I guess."

"Are you willing to do that?"

"If you're willing to trust me with the money," Roper said. "And you don't want to go and pick it up yourself."

"No," Orton said, "I'll trust you with it."

"We don't know exactly how much it's liable to be," Roper said. "Sure you want to trust me with that much temptation?"

"I can trust you, Andy," Orton said.

"What makes you say that?"

"I got a feeling about you," the other man said. "I have ever since I met you."

"Well, I don't know why that is," Roper said, "but I guess I appreciate it."

"Now that you're here, though," Orton said, "how about getting some work done?"

"Sure," Roper said. "What do you need?" *

"Go on out to the east pens and get me a count, will you?" Orton said. "I've got all the rest already."

"Use my boots," Orton said. "They're in the water closet."

"Thanks."

The boots didn't fit exactly, but they stayed on well enough. When Roper got to the pens, he saw the Fixx brothers there.

"Hey, Andy!" they greeted him, Stan slapping him on the back. "What're you doin' out here in the crap with the peons?"

"The boss sent me out for a count." The smell of manure was making his eyes water. "How do you stand this?"

"Just takes some gettin' used to, pal," Larry said. "Come on, we'll help you with that count."

Roper climbed up onto the corral so he could see, got himself comfortable on his perch. The cattle were standing easy as they began the count, but suddenly—after a few minutes—the beeves got agitated. Roper didn't know why until he heard it. It was probably the second shot he heard. The cows had heard the first one, and the third plucked at the left sleeve of his shirt. It surprised him, and as a result he fell into the pens.

Even as he fell, he thought, this must be how it happened to the other detective. He hit the ground and rolled, put his hands down to get to his feet, but slipped in the muck and manure. He reached for the gun Orton had given him, but it was gone. It must have fallen out of his belt when he landed, and was in the mud somewhere.

He probably wouldn't have been able to hold it anyway, his hands were so slick with manure.

He heard somebody yelling, and the steers began to buffet him. Cows weighed about twelve hundred pounds, but these steers went closer to fourteen or fifteen hundred. If he wasn't trampled, he could simply be crushed between two of them. He thought his best chance was to stay down. But that didn't seem to be the case, as one hoof struck him, and then another. He was wondering what to do—had never found himself in quite this situation before—when he suddenly felt hands on him, hauling him up and completely out of the pens.

The Fixx boys dumped him on the ground outside, where it was manure-free.

"That was close," Larry Fixx said with a big grin.

"Lucky we was there," Stan said.

"Yeah," Roper said, wringing his hands out to free them of some of the muck. "Lucky. How'd you happen to know where I was?"

"Larry saw you fall in and yelled," Stan said.

"I didn't fall in," Roper said, looking at his left arm. There was blood on his sleeve. "I was shot."

"Shot?" Larry said, looking puzzled.

"Somebody shot you?"

"Shot me right off my perch," Roper said. "You didn't hear it? The shots got the steers all riled up."

"I didn't hear nothin'," Larry said.

"Now that you mention it," Stan said, "I thought I heard somethin', but . . ."

"Jesus," Larry said as the blood started to trickle down Roper's arm, "are you okay?"

"Took a chunk of meat out of my arm," Roper said, "but I think I'll live."

"Come on, Larry," Stan said, "we better get him to the office."

Larry Fixx kicked the office door open and the brothers carried Roper in between them. Both Pete Orton and his wife looked at them, surprise on their faces, which were flushed. They'd obviously been having an argument.

"What happened?" Orton demanded.

"Somebody shot 'im," Larry said.

"What?"

"I told them I could walk," Roper said.

There was an old sofa against one wall that Roper had never sat on before. Too dirty.

"Sit him over there," Orton said, pointing to the sofa.

The brothers took Roper over there and dumped him on it. As they backed away, everyone could see the blood on Roper's arm.

"I better take a look at that," Louise Orton said.

She walked to the sofa, rolled Roper's sleeve up from the wound, and examined it.

"I don't see a bullet, but it needs to be cleaned," she said. She walked over to the water closet.

"Where did this happen?" Orton demanded.

"The east pens," Roper said.

"How?"

"Don't know," Roper said. "Somebody fired several shots. One hit me, knocked me into the pens. All the shots riled up the steers. I would have been crushed to death if not for these boys."

"Good thing we was there," Larry said.

"Same thing coulda happened to Andy that happened to that other fella," Stan said.

Louise returned with a basin of water, and a cloth. She sat next to Roper and began to clean his wound with firm, assured hands.

"Blood doesn't bother you?" Roper asked.

"I've seen plenty of it." She looked at her husband. "What are you going to do about this?"

"Send for a doctor," he said.

"I don't need one," Roper said. "Mrs. Orton is taking care of it fine."

"Then we need the police," Orton said.

"You know who they'll send," Roper said.

"I don't like those two detectives any more than you do," Orton said, "but we need to let the police know." Orton looked at the brothers. "One of you go and do that."

"Now?" Larry asked.

"Right now."

The two brothers exchanged a glance, and without another word, they decided which one would go. Stan turned and left.

As Mrs. Orton got the wound cleaned, she said, "I think this might need some stitches." Roper looked at her, and she met his eyes. "I can't do that."

"All right," Orton said. He looked at Larry Fixx. "Go get a doctor."

"Yes, sir."

He turned and left.

Orton looked at Roper. "You didn't see anybody?" he asked.

"I never even heard the first shot," Roper said. "I heard the echo of the second just as it hit me."

"Three shots," Orton said. "One man with a rifle?"

"Probably."

"That'll be up to the police to find out," Orton said.

"Damn it, first Mark Vaughn, now you."

"First Walt Henderson, you mean," Roper said.

"Walt Henderson?" Orton said, frowning. "But . . . but he fell."

"So did I," Roper pointed out, "but not without a little help."

49

Detectives Carradine and Cole arrived before the doctor did. Louise Orton had cleaned the wound and stopped the bleeding as well as she could.

"You wanna tell us what happened, Mr. Blake?" Carradine asked.

"I got shot."

They waited, but he said nothing else.

"That's it?" Carradine asked.

"That's all I know," Roper said. "I was workin' out in the pens and somebody took a shot at me."

"You hit bad?" Cole asked hopefully.

"They didn't miss," Roper said, indicating his arm, "but I'm not hit bad."

"You ever been shot before?" Carradine said.

"Nope," Roper lied. "Never."

"That's odd," Cole said.

"Is it?" Roper asked. "You ever been shot, Detective?"

"Yeah," Cole said.

"What about you, Carradine?"

"Yeah, once."

"Hmm," Roper said. "What about you, Pete?"

"No, never."

"There you go," Roper said, "Only half of us have ever been shot—well, before today."

"What about me?" Louise asked. "I've never been shot."

"There you go," Roper said, "only two out of five."

"Women don't count," Cole said.

The door opened and Larry Fixx entered with another man.

"Here's the doc, boss."

"What's your name, Doc?" Carradine asked.

The portly older man said, "Evans. And you?"

"Detective Carradine, Fort Worth Police."

"Police," Evans said. "I've always preferred a sheriff's office myself. Where's my patient?"

"Right there, Doc," Carradine said, pointing,

"Thank you."

Evans went over and sat next to Roper, began to examine him.

"What about Henderson, Detective?" Orton asked.

"Who?"

"Walt Henderson," Orton said. "He's the man who fell into the pens a while back, got trampled to death."

"Oh, him," Carradine said. "What about him?"

"Was he shot, too?"

Carradine looked at Cole.

"You don't know, do you?" Orton asked. "Nobody ever checked. They just assumed he fell."

"Why would somebody shoot him?" Carradine asked.

"I don't know," Orton said. "Why would somebody shoot Andy here?"

"I'd like to know that, too," Carradine said.

"Who cleaned this and stopped the bleeding?" the doctor asked.

"I did," Louise said. She was standing off to one side with her arms crossed.

"You did a fine job," the doctor said. "You should've been a nurse."

"Yes," she said, looking at her husband, "I should've been."

"How'd you get out of the pen?" Carradine asked.

"Larry and Stan pulled me out." Roper pointed at the brothers, also standing off to one side.

"Suppose you boys show us where this happened," Carradine said. He looked at Orton. "We'll have a look around and then come back. I suggest nobody leave, except the doctor."

"What about my wife?"

Carradine looked at her, then said, "Yeah, okay, she can go. But nobody else."

Who else was there? Roper thought. That left him and Orton in the office.

He had a decision to make.

After the doctor stitched him and left, and Louise Orton left with his thanks, Orton pulled a bottle of whiskey from his desk.

"Drink?"

"A big one."

Orton poured two drinks, passed one to Roper.

"What's going on?" Orton asked.

"What do you mean?"

"Andy—if that's your name—I knew when you came here that you were too smart to be looking for a job here. You ask a lot of questions, and you listen real well. You did a helluva job finding out what happened to Mark Vaughn, and given enough time, I'll bet you could find out what happened to Henderson. And now somebody tries to kill you, maybe the same way they killed him."

He walked to his desk and sat down. "Something's going on. Something's been going on for a while, but I tried to look the other way. I can't look the other way anymore."

50

"Talbot Roper," Roper said.

"I'm listening," Orton said.

"I'm a private detective. Normally I work out of Denver, but I was sent here to Fort Worth to look into what's been happening here at the stockyards."

"Sent by who?"

"The Pinkerton Agency."

"You're a Pinkerton?"

"No," Roper said, "I'm just doing this job for them."

"Who hired you?"

"Some people here in Fort Worth."

"The Cattleman's Club?"

"I can't tell you who the client is, Pete," Roper said. "I shouldn't even be telling you this, except that you've figured out that something isn't right."

Orton poured himself another drink.

"I knew you were too smart," he said. "Too smart for a job around here."

"You have a job around here," Roper pointed out.

"I'm not so smart," Orton said. "Not really."

"Smart enough to sniff me out," Roper said.

He stood up, crossed to Orton's desk, and held out his glass. Orton filled it.

"What do we do now?" Orton asked.

"Nothing," Roper said. "We go along as we have been. We don't tell the police who I am. Not yet anyway."

"You don't trust them?"

"I don't like them," Roper said. "To tell you the truth, I don't trust anybody."

"Not even me?"

"I have to trust you now," Roper said. "You could do me and my investigation considerable harm."

"I won't."

"I hope not," Roper said.

They studied each other for a few moments, and then Orton said, "How much—how deep did your investigation go?"

"You mean do I know about you and Nancy Ransom?" Roper asked.

"Yep," Orton said, "that's what I mean. I guess when you found that out, it made me a suspect."

"Not really," Roper said. "Cheating on one's wife doesn't make a man a criminal. But when I found out who owned that little house you use . . ."

Orton leaned back in his chair, as if he was afraid of the answer, and asked, "Who?"

"Brewster."

"What?"

"How did you find that house?"

"Nancy found it," he said.

"How did you meet Nancy?"

"In the Bullshead," Orton said. "I went there with some fellas, and she approached me."

It sounded to Roper like Orton had been set up to meet Nancy.

"Who took you to the Bullshead?" Roper asked.

"A couple of young fellas named Joe Roberts and Dick Kelly."

"And where are they now?"

"They don't work here anymore," Orton said.

"Why not?"

"They quit."

"After you started seeing Nancy?"

Orton hesitated, then said, "Yes."

"What are you thinking, Pete?" Roper asked.

Orton rubbed his hands over his face and said, "I was set up?"

Roper nodded.

"Nancy?"

Roper nodded again.

"But somebody must have put her up to it," Roper said.

"Who?"

"Brewster owns the house," Roper said. "He bought it from Mannerly."

"Old Man Mannerly?" Orton said. "He's in on this, too?"

"Maybe not," Roper said. "All he did was sell a house."

"Oh, wait, wait," Orton said, "So I was set up . . . but for what?"

"Pillow talk," Roper said.

"Pillow . . ."

"After you and Nancy have sex, what happens?"

"We lie together and . . . talk."

"About what?"

Orton shrugged and said, "Everything."

"Your personal life?"

"Yes."

"And your business?"

Orton hesitated, then said, "Yeah."

"Is that when the troubles started?"

"I think so," Orton said, Then he was struck with the realization of what that meant. His eyes widened. "You mean all of this sabotage has been . . . my fault?"

"Maybe not all of it," Roper said, "but some of it."

"Sonofabitch!"

"Are you in love with Nancy?"

"No," he said immediately, "it's never been about love with her. I just . . . have to have her."

"I understand that."

"Now I want to wring her scrawny neck!" Orton said angrily.

"Not yet," Roper said. "Now that we suspect her, we have to use her."

"How?"

"By giving her false information and seeing if it gets back to Brewster. Or whoever is behind her."

A flurry of emotions crossed Orton's features and then he said, "Eddie Parker!"

"Who is he?"

"A two-bit hustler," he said. "I saw him with Nancy—I've seen him with her over and over, and she insists there's nothing between them."

"But she's having some of the Bullshead customers rolled for the money," Roper said. "For that she's got to have a partner."

"Parker."

"Maybe," Roper said. "I'll have to look into him."

Roper was starting to think that maybe Nancy Ransom had more than one thing going for her. Orton described Eddie Parker as a hustler, but maybe the same word applied to her.

51

Roper felt it might be time to come out from behind "Andy Blake." He felt he could trust the Fixx brothers, as he had trusted Pete Orton, who seemed genuinely ashamed of himself. Roper prided himself on being a judge of character. If Orton was acting, and lying to him, he was one of the best he'd ever seen.

There had been something he didn't like about Brewster. He needed to look deeper into the man's background, and his life. The same with Eddie Parker. He needed to meet him, and learn more about him.

"Pete," he said before the detectives came back, "what's going on with you and your wife?"

"We just . . . drifted apart."

"Is she seeing anyone behind your back?"

Orton's eyes widened and said, "I don't think so."

"She's a beautiful woman," Roper said. "If she's not getting attention from you, she might be getting it from somewhere else."

"I—I don't know . . ."

"You mind if I try to find out?" Roper asked.

"No," Orton said, "no, I don't mind. In fact, I'd like to know."

"All right then—"

At that moment the door opened and the two detectives came back in.

"Your men are outside," Carradine said to Orton. "Do you want them—"

"No, no," Orton said, standing up. "I'll tell them to go back to work."

He came around the desk and went out the door.

Carradine and Cole stared at Roper.

"What did you find?" he asked.

"Not much," Carradine said. "There are a lot of points from where the shots could've been fired."

"Mmm . . ."

"What's on your mind?" Cole asked.

"I think we need to talk," Roper said.

"About what?"

"A lot of things," Roper said, "but I want to talk to your boss, as well."

"We're investigating this thing—" Cole started.

"I'll talk to you two," Roper said, "and the marshal."

"When?" Carradine asked.

Roper thought a moment.

"Tomorrow morning," he said finally. "I'll come to the police station at nine a.m."

"Not worried about losing your job here?" Carradine asked.

"Not anymore," Roper said.

"Okay," Carradine said, "tomorrow morning."

The detectives left the office. Orton did not come back in right away.

Roper had to decide who else he was going to reveal himself to. He'd have to talk to Kalish about it, and he wanted to do that before he talked to the detectives and the marshal.

And maybe he'd move out of the rooming house and into a decent hotel.

Orton came back in after a few moments.

"Did you tell them?" he asked.

"Not yet," Roper said. "I'm going to talk to them and their boss tomorrow morning."

"Meanwhile," Orton asked, "what do I do?"

"Well," Roper said, "if I was you, I'd start looking for a new assistant."

After he left the stockyard, Roper thought about going to the Cattleman's Club. It was almost six, but he was sure a lot of the members would be there having dinner. In the end, he decided to do just that.

He caught a cab and had it drive him to the Cattleman's Club.

The doorman was not Lester, but another man.

"I need to see Mr. Kalish," he said.

"And your name?"

He hesitated, then said, "Andy Blake."

"Does he know who you are, sir?"

"Yes, he does."

"Wait here, please."

Roper waited. Several men entered and others left; none that he knew, though. The doorman returned and said, "Follow me, please."

Once again he entered the building and followed someone down a hall. This time the doorman took him to the same room where he had met earlier with Kalish.

"Mr. Blake, sir," the doorman said.

"Thank you, Tony," Kalish said. "That's all."

The doorman left and closed the door.

"Mr. Roper," Kalish said. "What brings you here?"

"Somebody tried to kill me today," Roper said. "I think the cat might be out of the bag."

"Who . . . who do you think did that?"

"I don't know," Roper said. "Tell me about your colleagues."

"Colleagues?"

"The men we had dinner with," Roper said. "The men you partnered with in hiring the Pinkertons."

"Oh," Kalish said, "well, Halfwell and Mannerly have been in the cattle business a long time."

"They seem to be . . . past it, if you'll excuse me for saying."

"No, you're right," Kalish said. "They are a bit . . . vacant sometimes."

"So it falls to the other three of you to make the decisions, right?"

"That's right," Kalish said.

"Tell me about Arnold."

"He's a follower," Kalish said. "He'll back whoever's got the floor, really."

"And who has the floor most of the time?" Roper asked.

"Brewster."

"Why?" Roper asked. "Why him and not you?"

"He's the youngest," Kalish said, "the strongest, I suppose."

"Why do you let him take the lead?"

"He's also very smart."

"Was he in favor of hiring the Pinkertons?"

"Well . . . not at first," Kalish said.

"Why did he give in?"

"I'm not sure," Kalish said. "I think Mannerly and Halfwell may have woken up that day and sided with me."

"And Arnold?"

"He sided with Brewster."

"So when Brewster changed his mind?"

"Arnold changed as well."

"Did you ever tell any of them about me?"

"No," Kalish said. "I kept to my agreement with the Pinkertons."

"Brewster had a feeling about me, though," Roper said. "He pretty much told me so. Did he mention it to you?"

"No, never."

"I wonder why not."

"I'm sorry," Kalish said, "do you want a drink?"

"No, thanks."

"Why all the questions about Brewster?"

Roper didn't answer.

"You don't think that Brewster . . . that he's behind any of this, do you?"

"What would he gain from keeping Eastern interests out of Fort Worth?" Roper asked.

"I don't know," Kalish said. "We need the influx of that money—"

"What if he had another investor, somebody else who was interested?"

"I don't know of anyone else—"

"Maybe that's the point," Roper said. "You don't know of anyone else's interest, but he does."

"Well, if he manages to convince certain people that the problems here are insurmountable . . . yes, I guess he could make his own deal with someone."

"And cut out you, Arnold, Mannerly, and Halfwell."

"Yes."

"He'd become a very rich man, wouldn't he?"

"He would—he's already a rich man, but he'd be . . . even richer."

Roper nodded.

"I can't believe it's him."

"Well," Roper said, "we don't know that for a fact yet, but I'll be looking at him."

"Yes, all right."

"But it's important you say nothing to him," Roper added.

"I understand. Are you going to talk to anyone else? I mean, about who you really are?"

Roper decided to conceal the truth. "So far it's still just you and me, Harold."

"All right," Kalish said. "Thanks for coming by and letting me know what's going on."

"Sure."

Roper turned to leave.

"Mr. Roper," Kalish said, "you said somebody tried to kill you. Were you hurt?"

"A bullet nicked me," Roper said, "and I fell into some manure."

"I thought I smelled . . ." Kalish said, waving his hand.

"Yeah, I tried to clean up at work. I'll need to take a bath tonight. A long bath."

52

Roper left the Cattleman's Club and went directly to his rooming house. He had missed dinner, but Mrs. Varney agreed to draw him a bath—wrinkling her nose at him the whole time. He had a feeling she was doing it for her own benefit, not his.

He soaked in a bath until he was sure the smell of manure was gone. He managed to do it without getting the bandage on his arm wet, so the stitches the doctor had put there remained intact.

When he was finished, he dried off, pulled his trousers on, and walked to his room. He entered, put on a clean shirt, but didn't button it. He was not going out again. He just wanted to be comfortable.

He walked to his window and stared out at the darkness of Hell's Half Acre. In the morning he was going to register at a decent hotel before going to the police station. He wasn't going to tell anyone where he was staying.

Idly, he wondered what had become of Dol Bennett. Had she gone back to Chicago? Or was she still hanging around Fort Worth?

He thought he still smelled manure and wondered if he'd need to take another bath when he got to his new hotel. But then he realized his clothes were on the floor in a corner. He couldn't put them in the hall, so he decided to go downstairs and see if he could find a bag to put them in until he could get them washed.

He buttoned his shirt and left his room, went down the stairs to the main floor. Nobody was around. They were either in their rooms, or out of the house.

He waited a few moments for his eyes to adjust to the darkness, then made his way through the dining room to the kitchen. He got to the door and thought he heard somebody inside. He didn't have a gun with him, but he didn't really expect any danger there. He opened the swinging door as quietly as he could. He heard heavy breathing and grunting, saw two figures intertwined against a wall of the kitchen. He realized that the girl, Lauren, was there, having sex with a man—maybe one of the boarders. He had her up against the wall and was thrusting himself into her, his bare buttocks clenching and unclenching. Her eyes opened at that moment and then widened when she saw him watching them. He withdrew, letting the door close. What they were doing was their business, not his.

He went back upstairs.

About twenty minutes later there was a light knocking on his door. He opened it, saw a fully dressed but tousled-looking Lauren in the hall.

"Hello, Lauren."

"Mr. Blake . . ." she said breathlessly.

"Don't worry," he said, "I'm not going to tell anyone what I saw."

"You're not?" She looked hopeful.

"On one condition."

"Oh." It appeared she thought she knew what the condition would be.

"I need a bag."

"A bag?" She frowned.

"A sack, really," he said. "Or even some brown paper. I have some . . . clothes to wrap up."

"We have brown paper."

"Good," he said. "Bring me some and your secret is safe with me."

"Really?" she asked. "That's all?"

"That's it."

"Now?"

"Yes, now."

"I'll bring it right up," she said excitedly.

It had been about five minutes when there was a knock on his door again. He opened it and she thrust some brown paper and some twine into his hands.

"You can wrap up the clothes in this," she said.

"Fine, thanks."

She stood there.

"Anything else?" he asked.

"Mrs. Varney," she said, "if she found out . . . well, she'd skin me alive."

"And the man, too, I bet."

"Oh, yes," she said. "She wants me to stay away from her boarders."

"Well, don't worry," he said. "Like I told you before, your secret is safe with me."

"Oh, thank you, sir."

"I'll see you at breakfast, then."

"Yes, sir," she said, "and it'll be extra good. I promise."

She hurried quietly down the hall.

He wrapped his smelly clothes in brown paper, tied the bundle up right, and tossed it in a corner.

He tried to turn in then, but his arm ached, and he thought again about somebody trying to shoot him. He wondered if they were trying to kill Talbot Roper or Andy Blake?

He got up, shoved the back of a wooden chair underneath the doorknob, then set a pitcher on the windowsill where someone trying to get in would have to knock it down.

Reasonably secure, he went back to bed with his gun beneath his pillow.

This time he fell asleep.

53

In the morning he was at the table for breakfast and received special treatment from Lauren, who graced him with a broad smile every time she came by. He was afraid it only served to make Mrs. Varney suspicious.

He noticed there were some faces missing, including Embry and Rickman. Catlin was still there, eating breakfast right next to him.

"What happened to our happy crew?" Roper asked.

"What do you mean?"

"I see some faces missing."

"They moved on."

"Embry and Rickman?"

"They left at the same time."

Roper wondered if they had quit their jobs at the stockyards, as well.

"You missed dinner again last night," Catlin said. "Good food."

"Yeah," Roper said, "I had some things to do."

Roper studied Catlin for a moment, wondering if he was the man who was in the kitchen with Lauren last night.

"What have you been up to?" he asked.

"Just trying to get my practice up and running," Catlin said. "You don't need a lawyer, do you?"

"Not yet," Roper said.

"Well, keep me in mind."

After breakfast, Roper pulled Catlin aside and said, "I'm leaving today."

"You, too?" Catlin asked. "What's happening here? Where are you going?"

"I'll still be in town," Roper said, "but I'm finding a new place."

"Look," Catlin said, reaching into his pocket, "I just got business cards made up. Contact me when you find a place. We'll have dinner together."

"I'll do that," Roper said, and they shook hands.

After that, Roper settled up with Mrs. Varney, who simply sniffed when he said he was leaving, and then he walked out the front door with his carpetbag.

Roper did not have time to check into a hotel before nine o'clock, so he went directly to the police station. He presented himself to the sergeant at the front desk and asked for Detective Carradine. He wondered why the Fort Worth Police Department had a marshal in charge rather than a police chief.

"Are you moving in?" Carradine asked when he came out.

"Out," Roper said, "then in. I just didn't have time to find a hotel before nine."

"Yeah, well, follow me," Carradine said.

He led Roper down a hall to a door that said, MARSHAL B. GATES.

Inside were Marshal Gates, seated behind his desk, and Detective Cole, sitting across from him.

"Have a seat, Mr. Blake," the marshal said. "I understand you have something to tell us."

There was only one other chair. Roper took it, and Carradine stood.

"First," Roper said, "my name's not Andy Blake. It's Talbot Roper."

Cole sat up in his chair.

"The private detective?"

"That's right."

"You've heard of him?" the marshal asked Cole.

"Well, Jesus," Cole said, "I thought everybody in law enforcement had heard of him. He used to be a Pinkerton, but left to open his own agency. He's pretty much considered to be the best private detective in the country."

Gates looked at Carradine.

"You?"

"I've heard of him," Carradine said, with less enthusiasm than his partner.

"All right," Gates said, "before we all get too excited, can you prove you are who you say you are?"

Roper produced his credentials. Gates examined them, then passed them on to Cole. Finally, they went to Carradine and back to Roper.

"All right, Mr. Roper," Gates said, "why the subterfuge?"

"I've been sent in by the Pinkertons to find out who's trying to sabotage the stockyards."

"They don't think we can do the job?" Gates asked.

"Hell," Carradine said, "*we* don't think we can do the job."

Gates scowled at his detective.

"All I mean is—" Carradine started.

"Yes, we know what you mean, Detective," Gates said.

"You joined the Pinkertons again?" Cole asked. He was looking at Roper in a totally different light than the way he had looked at "Andy Blake."

"Just for this job," Roper said.

"So," Gates said, "have you solved the case? Is that why you've come out into the light?"

"No," Roper said, "but yesterday somebody tried to kill me, so I must be getting close."

"So why are you here?" Gates asked. "To tell us what you have? Or to ask for help?"

Roper didn't want to give them all he had, so he said, "To ask for help."

That seemed to mollify Gates and Carradine, and excite Cole.

"What can we do for you?" Gates asked.

"What do you know about a man named Eddie Parker?"

"A bottom feeder," Carradine said right away. "Preys on the weak, because he hasn't got the guts to go any higher. He's a tall drink of water who is all ears." Carradine held his hands to his ears and waved them. "Literally all ears."

"What's your interest in Parker?" Cole asked.

"Do you fellas know who Nancy Ransom is?" Roper asked.

"No," Carradine said, and Cole shook his head. Oddly, Gates did not respond.

"She's a saloon girl at the Bullshead Saloon," Roper said.

"Not my place," Carradine said. "What's her game?"

"Apparently," Roper said, "she's working with Parker to have some Bullshead customers rolled."

"That's right," Cole said, "we've had some complaints about that, but nobody's mentioned her."

"You sure she's working with Parker?" Gates asked.

"Positive," Roper said. "They tried to have me rolled when I first got here, remember?"

"Ah," Carradine said, "the two you killed in your first hotel." Roper was not surprised that the two detectives had uncovered that bit of information.

"Right," Roper said. "I had talked to Nancy earlier. And I've talked to her since. She seemed to sense that I wasn't who I said I was and agreed to leave me alone."

"You think she's the one who tried to have you killed?" Carradine asked.

"Or Parker," Roper said, "unless he took the shot himself."

"Never happen," Carradine said. "He doesn't have the nerve, or the ability."

"So he hired it out," Roper said. "Who does that kind of work?"

"In Fort Worth?" Cole asked. "You can't swing a dead cat by the tail without hitting somebody who thinks he's a crack shot and would hire himself out."

"Great," Roper said. "I was hoping you could narrow it down to two or three for me."

"Afraid you'll have to do your own legwork on that, Mr. Roper."

"Well, I'm going to find Parker and talk to him," Roper said. "I'm just letting you know."

"Try not to kill him," Gates said.

"I'll do my best."

"Or the girl," Carradine said.

"Oh yeah," Roper said, "I'll be talking to her, too."

"Well," Gates said, "we appreciate you coming out from behind your disguise and letting us know, Mr. Roper."

"Always ready to cooperate with the local law," Roper said, standing up.

"Detective Carradine will walk you out."

"I can do that—" Cole said, starting to stand up.

"Sit!" Gates barked, and Cole fell back into his chair.

Roper followed Carradine to the front of the building.

Out on the steps Carradine said, "I'm not as big a fan of yours as my partner is, Roper."

"I could tell."

"But if there's anything else I can do to help, let me know."

"Actually . . ." Roper said.

"Yeah?"

"Do you know where I could get a good suit?"

54

Roper thought about checking into one of the more upscale hotels, but he finally settled on something less ostentatious but still high end. It was called the Colonial Palace, and it was a few blocks from the White Elephant.

Carradine had given him some suggestions for a place he could get a suit, but Roper decided to go straight to the horse's mouth, the dapperest man he knew of in Fort Worth.

Luke Short.

He pounded on the front door of the White Elephant until somebody opened it. It was a man with an apron, apparently a bartender.

"We ain't open yet."

"I'm here to see Luke Short," Roper said, "not to drink or gamble."

"Who are you?"

"Talbot Roper," the detective said. "I'm a friend of his."

"Roper," the bartender said. He seemed to be searching for something in his head, then he nodded. "Yeah, okay. Come on in."

The White Elephant was not just empty, it was cavernous with nobody in it. All the tables had their chairs stacked up on them.

"Grab a seat and wait here," the bartender said. "I'll get him."

"Thanks."

"There's coffee behind the bar."

Roper walked behind the bar and poured himself a cup. Then took a chair down from a table and sat.

The bartender came down and said, "Luke'll be right down."

He then disappeared somewhere in the back.

Short appeared moments later, came down the stairs looking as dapper as ever. If he'd had to dress quickly, he'd done a hell of a job.

"This better be good," Short said. "I don't get that much time to spend with my wife."

"Sorry," Roper said, "you said you were available to help."

"I am," Short said. "Let me get a cup of coffee."

Short went behind the bar, came back with a cup. Roper had taken down a chair for him, and he sat in it, crossed one leg over a knee.

"What's up?"

"I had to come out from behind my disguise," Roper said.

"So you're Talbot Roper again?"

"That's right."

Short studied him critically for a moment.

"You need a suit."

"I do."

"I'll tell you where to go."

"Thanks."

"What else?"

"Eddie Parker," Roper said.

"Scum," Short said, "but small-time scum."

"I'm thinking maybe he's moving up," Roper said. "Know anything about a gal named Nancy Ransom?"

"I do, actually. Smart lady. I wish she'd come work here."

"Did you make an offer?"

"I did," Short said. "There's somethin' holdin' her to the Bullshead. That's all I can figure."

"What if I told you she was involved with Parker?" Short asked.

"I'd say balderdash," Short said. "She's too classy for him."

"Well, they're working together," Roper said. "I know that for a fact. What do you say to that?"

"If Parker and Nancy are doing something together, I'd say Nancy is running the show."

"Now that is interesting."

They both sipped their coffee.

"Okay, one more thing," Roper said. "The bunch at the Cattleman's Club."

"Ah," Short said, "they run the town."

"You know any of them?"

"I've played poker a time or two with a fella named Arnold," Short said, "but that's about it. I don't cross paths with the rest of them much."

"What do you hear?"

"Nothing helpful, I don't think," Short said. "Mannerly and Halfwell are past it. Just too old. All they do is supply money."

"And the others?"

"It seems that a man named Brewster runs the show," Short said, "but I hear he couldn't do it without Harold Kalish."

"That's interesting."

"Why?" Short asked. "Did one of them hire you? They did, didn't they? Which one? Which one hired you?"

"Thanks for talking to me, Luke."

"You're not gonna tell me, are you?"

Roper got up, turned to leave, then turned back.

"Oh yeah," he said, "about that suit—"

55

Roper looked at himself in the mirror, liked the cut and fit of the coat.

"When can this be ready?" he asked.

"Since you're a friend of Mr. Short's," the little tailor said, "later today, at four."

"Seriously?"

"We aim to please."

"I wish my tailor in Denver thought that way."

They removed the suit and Roper got back into his "Andy Blake" clothes—hopefully for the last time. The clerk at the hotel looked at him askance until he produced the money for the room. It would have been the same with the tailor if he had not involved Luke's name, and if Luke had not sent instructions with a messenger for the tailor to treat Roper the same way the tailor would have treated Luke.

"And," the tailor said, "I can make another in brown, if you like, now that I have the measurements."

"That'd be fine," Roper said.

"Yes, sir," the tailor said. "Excellent. You can pick them up at five."

"Thank you."

He strapped on his gun—which, until that day, had resided at the bottom of his carpetbag—and left the tailor shop.

He had about six hours before the suits would be ready. He didn't want to go and see Nancy until he was wearing one of the suits, so he decided to go looking for Eddie Parker.

He went back to the place where he'd seen Nancy Ransom on the street that one day. She had come from around the corner, so it was possible that Eddie Parker lived on that street. Of course, he could have lived blocks from there, but since she was walking, not riding in a cab, he felt certain Parker lived just a block or two away.

He decided to wait. It wasn't noon yet, and the Eddie Parker who had been described to him by several people did not strike him as an early riser.

So he decided to just stand there and wait for Eddie to walk by.

Hopefully.

There was a general store nearby so Roper got himself a bag of rock candy and stood on the corner popping pieces into his mouth. Although he had a sweet tooth, he did not give in to it very often, and usually when he did, it was with a piece of pie.

He was working his way through the bag while a small boy came up and stood next to him, watching him. He thought about giving the boy the bag, but decided that he really wanted it for himself.

"Go away," he told the boy, who seemed all of five years old.

The boy just stared, his mouth slightly open.

"Where's your mother?"

The boy pointed. Roper looked, saw a dress shop. No telling how long the woman would be in there.

He looked down at the boy.

"You know, I'd change corners," he said, "but I was here first."

The boy stared.

He decided to give the boy one piece. He took one and held it out. The boy grabbed it and stuffed it into his mouth, but continued to stare. Before long he was also drooling.

"Wipe your mouth, kid," Roper said, popping another piece into his own mouth.

There was still half a bag of candy when a pair of ears walked by him.

He was surprised that the man came from another direction and turned into the side street, rather than coming from that street.

"Parker," Roper said as the man with the huge ears walked by.

He looked down at the kid, who had not moved, and finally handed him the bag. The boy took it, as if he had known all along he'd get it.

"Enjoy it," Roper said, and followed Eddie Parker.

56

Roper turned the corner, prepared to follow Parker for however long it took. He was surprised when the man simply crossed the street and went up a flight of stairs along the side of a building. He watched as the man unlocked a door and went inside.

Very convenient.

He walked to the stairs and went up slowly, giving Parker time to get settled inside. When he reached the door, he knocked.

The man with the big ears swung the door open and stared at Roper.

"Yeah?"

"Eddie Parker?"

"Who wants to know?"

This was the easiest part, because he was used to dealing with men like this. And in this instance, he could just be himself.

Roper stiff-armed the man back into the room, and followed.

Parker staggered back, his arms windmilling as he tried

to keep his balance. But he hit a chair and went over backward.

Roper closed the door behind him.

"What the hell—" Parker said, getting to his feet.

"We're going to have a talk, Eddie."

"Who the hell are you?" Parker demanded. "Get the hell out—"

"Shut up!"

Parker did, but just for a moment.

"Wait a minute, you can't talk to me like that," he said. He flicked his eyes to one side. Roper looked and saw the man's gun sitting on the top of a table.

"Don't try it," Roper said.

"What?"

"The gun," Roper said. "Don't try for it."

"What the hell—" Parker started, but he stopped himself. "Uh, can I get up?"

"Sure," Roper said, "get to your feet."

Parker got up from the floor, but couldn't help himself and once again looked at his gun.

"Okay," Roper said. He strode across the room and picked the gun up off the table. He put it in his pocket and looked at Parker.

"Okay," he said again, "that temptation is gone. Now we can talk."

"About what?"

"About you and Nancy Ransom."

"I don't know who that is."

"Very bad lie, Eddie," Roper said. "I know the two of you work together. And for a while I thought she worked for you. But now I know that you work for her."

"Well, that's—what?" Parker looked puzzled.

"You roll drunks for her," Roper said. "That is, you find men who will roll drunks—or customers—for her."

"Are you the law?" Parker asked suspiciously.

"I'm a private detective, Eddie," Roper said. "From Denver."

"So what are you doin' here?"

"I'm trying to find out who's doing damage to the stockyards."

"The stockyards?" Parker said. "I don't know nothin' about that."

"Are you sure?"

"I mean, I heard about some things—there was a fire recently. Right?"

"That's right."

"But I don't know nothin' about that."

"You just rob people."

"Well . . . yeah," Parker said. "We rob people who have lots of money." He shrugged. "They don't miss it. Nobody gets hurt."

"Except when they do."

"Well . . . sometimes . . ."

"Sometimes somebody dies," Roper said, "like the two men you sent after me."

"What? You?"

"I'm one of the men Nancy picked out," Roper said, "only that was a big mistake. I killed the two men you sent after me."

"That was you?"

"That's right."

"Look," Parker said, "that wasn't me. None of that was my idea. Y-You're right, I work for Nancy. It's all her doin'."

"Can you tell me why she's sleeping with Pete Orton?" Roper asked.

"What? Who? I don't know who that is."

Roper could tell from the look on the man's face that he was telling the truth.

Eddie Parker was just what he appeared to be, a low-level thief. Could it really be that Nancy Ransom was just trying to make some money on the side?

"What is she doing with you?"

"What?"

"Nancy?" Roper said. "What does she want with you?"

Insulted, Parker sort of adjusted his collar and said, "Well . . . I'm good at what I do."

"Which is?"

"Thievery."

"And why is she interested in thievery?"

"You really askin' me?"

"I am."

Parker shrugged and said, "I think she's bored."

"Or," Roper said, "she's following somebody else's instructions."

"What?"

Roper was getting tired of talking to Parker. He obviously knew nothing and was just going to keep asking, "What?"

"Okay, Eddie," Roper said. "We're done."

He turned and walked to the door.

"Wait!" Parker said.

Roper turned. "Yes?"

"What about my gun?"

"I'll leave it at the bottom of the steps."

"Um, well . . . okay."

"But there is one more thing."

"What's that?"

"Don't mention this meeting to Nancy," Roper said. "If I find out you did, I'll be back."

"Um, okay."

"Don't make me come back, Eddie."

"I won't," Parker said, "I swear!"

"Good-bye, Eddie."

"You didn't tell me your name!" Parker called out as Roper opened the door.

"No," Roper said, "I didn't."

57

Roper's intention when he left Eddie Parker's rooms was to go and see Nancy next. But as he turned the corner and started walking down the street, he decided to go and see another woman first.

But before seeing either woman—Louise Orton or Nancy Ransom—he needed a few other things.

A bath, a shave, and his new suits.

In the bathtub, Roper kept his gun nearby, hanging on the back of a nearby chair, within reach. Somebody had tried to kill him once, and they might try again. Or maybe the shooting had been a warning. Either way he was determined to keep his own gun on him, or within reach.

He'd had his shave—and a haircut to boot—followed by this bath. Once he picked up his new suits from the tailor, which he would do next, he'd feel like himself again. No more "Andy Blake," and more important, no more manure.

* * *

Roper had never been to Pete Orton's house, but because he worked in the man's office, he knew what his address was.

He also knew that Orton, being the man he was, would still be at work. Roper wanted to talk to Louise Orton alone. He needed to know if *she* knew about her husband's infidelity, if she herself was cheating, and if she had anything to do with the sabotage. There had to be someone working on the inside.

The Ortons lived in a two-family wood frame house in a pretty middle-class neighborhood, probably equidistant from Hell's Half Acre and the high-class saloons like the White Elephant.

He mounted the porch and knocked on the door. Louise Orton answered fairly quickly, frowned when she saw him.

"Can I help you?"

It was obvious she didn't recognize him with his haircut, shave, and new suit. He took off the flat-brimmed hat he was wearing and held it in his hands.

"Mrs. Orton, it's me, Andy Blake."

"Mr. Blake?" she frowned. "Well, it is you. But . . . you look so different."

"I can explain," he said. "May I come in?"

"Of course."

She let him in, led him to a comfortably, but not expensively, furnished living room, where she turned to face him. She was wearing a simple, high-necked dress that molded itself to her slender body. She was lovely, with a long, graceful neck and breasts that looked like teacups.

"Shouldn't you be at work?" she asked. "Did my husband send you?"

"Mrs. Orton," he said, "my name is not really Andy Blake."

"It isn't?"

"No, ma'am," he said. "My name is Talbot Roper. I'm a private detective from Denver, on loan to the Pinkerton Agency."

She stared at him, then said, "I don't understand."

"Can we sit down?"

"Yes, please."

He sat down in an armchair, while she took a seat on one end of the sofa.

"I'm sure you're aware of all the incidents that have been occurring at the stockyards these past few months?" he said.

"Yes, of course," she said. "Leading up to the recent fire."

"Yes. Well, I've been sent here to investigate. I came in as 'Andy Blake,' to try to get some information without anyone knowing who I am."

"I see," she said. "You were lying to us."

"I was undercover," he said.

She smiled without humor and said, "Well, whatever you want to call it."

"I was doing my job, Mrs. Orton."

"So I assume you are also doing your job with this visit?" she asked. "What can I do for you, Mr. . . . Roper, is it?"

"Yes, Roper."

Louise had folded her arms across her chest, but now she dropped them, as well as the stern look on her face.

"I suppose there's no reason for me to be rude," she said. "Can I offer you something? A drink? Or coffee?"

"Coffee would be fine." He felt having coffee would soften the mood even more. He often accepted offers of coffee or tea in these instances for just that reason.

"Excuse me." She went to the kitchen and was there for quite a while. If he hadn't been able to hear her puttering around in there, he might have thought she'd gone out the back door. Roper was wearing his holster, having left his shoulder rig back in Denver. He eased his weight onto his left hip, giving himself better access to the gun on his right, just in case.

Louise finally reappeared, carrying a tray that contained a pot of coffee, two cups, and a tray of cookies. She set it down on the table in front of the sofa.

"Sugar? Milk?"

"Just black, thanks."

She poured out two cups, took hers black as well, and then sat back.

"Well," she said, "suppose you tell me why you've come to see me today? Could it be that you suspect my husband of being involved in these incidents?"

"I actually did suspect him for a while," he said.

"What changed your mind?"

"Working with him for as long as I did," Roper said. "I decided he was trying too hard to make things work. I can't see him doing anything to sabotage the company."

"He is a hard worker," she said. "Some nights he doesn't come home till very late."

"And you?"

"What about me?"

"What do you do with yourself when he's not home?"

"My God," she said calmly. She set her cup down, put her hands in her lap. "You suspect me of something, don't you?"

"I wouldn't say that," he answered. "Let's just say I'm curious about what you do with your time."

"Maybe you should be concerned with my husband's extracurricular activities."

"Does he have some?"

"Oh yes," she said. "He's not as pristine as you seem to think he is. Not while he's been cheating on me."

"So you know about that."

"And, it seems, so do you," she said. "So why don't you talk to that saloon girl he's been sleeping with?"

"I intend to," he said. "In fact, it's my next stop."

For the first time she seemed a bit shaken. When she used her hand to push some hair away from her face, there was a slight tremor.

"I don't know how he could do that to us."

"Mrs. Orton," Roper said, "I'll repeat my question. What about you?"

"You mean have I been cheating?" she asked. "You don't know? Haven't you been following me?"

"As a matter of fact, I haven't," Roper said, "so feel free to lie to me."

She sat silently for a moment, then said, "I'm not a nun, Mr. Roper. I've had my share of lovers, but only when I realized Pete was . . . cheating on me. I know, I sound like the pitiful wife . . ."

"Why don't you leave?"

"And go where?"

He decided not to answer. He was not a marriage counselor. Maybe if they stayed together long enough, they'd work something out.

"These lovers, Louise," he said, "have you been with anyone you may have said something to? Something about the stockyards?"

"You mean have I revealed any secrets through pillow talk?"

"That's exactly what I mean."

"I don't know anything about my husband's business, Mr. Roper," she said. "He's not home long enough to tell me anything. So no, I haven't told anybody anything. I'm not the person you should be suspicious of."

"That's okay," he said, "I have plenty of others."

He stood up. She didn't.

"If you don't mind," she said, "I'll let you find your own way out."

"I don't mind, Mrs. Orton," he said, and left.

58

Roper was of the opinion that neither of the Ortons was deliberately involved in the stockyard incidents. However, that didn't mean that Pete Orton still didn't tell Nancy Ransom things during pillow talk that could have been used. So his next step was to talk to Nancy. That meant going to the Bullshead for the first time as himself.

He found a cab after a few blocks and had it take him to the saloon and gambling hall.

As he entered, the place was as busy as ever. The stuffy smell of stale beer and sweat hit him as soon as he walked through the batwings, and he suddenly longed for a cold beer at the White Elephant. He'd had just about enough of Hell's Half Acre.

He walked to the bar, found himself a spot, and ordered a beer. Looking around, he saw no sign of Nancy. He wondered if he'd frightened Eddie Parker sufficiently to keep him from running to Nancy Ransom.

The bartender brought him a beer that looked both flat and warm. "Nancy around?" Roper asked.

"She ain't come down yet."

"But she's working tonight?"

"Oh, yeah."

"Okay, thanks."

He left the beer there without touching it. He'd come to a decision, and walked across the floor, dodging customers and working girls. He went up the stairs and walked to Nancy's door. He knocked.

"Who is it?" she called.

"Me," he said.

She opened the door, saying, "Me, who—" and stopped short when she saw him. "Hey, you can't be—"

He pushed her into the room, stepped in after her, and closed the door.

The bartender watched Roper walk up the stairs, saw him push his way into Nancy's room.

"Hey, Willie," he said to a man standing at the end of the bar.

"Yeah?"

"Watch the bar for a minute."

"Really?" Willie asked, excited.

"Yeah."

"Can I have a drink?" Willie asked, moving around behind the bar.

"Yeah," the bartender said, "one."

He walked to the back of the room to his boss's office and knocked.

"What the hell do you think you're doin'?" Nancy demanded.

"We have to have a talk."

"I thought we agreed to leave each other alone."

"That was when you thought my name was Andy Blake," he said.

"And your name's not Andy Blake?"

"No."

"Okay," she said, "okay, I'll bite . . . what is your name?"

"Talbot Roper."

She stared at him, waiting for more, and when it didn't come, she said, "So? Who's Talbot Roper?"

"A private detective."

"A what?"

"Pinkerton."

That word she knew.

"What are you talkin' about?" she demanded. "You're a goddamned Pinkerton?"

"I'm working with the Pinkertons," he corrected her.

"What's the difference?"

"Probably none to you," he said.

"What do you want?"

"I'm in Fort Worth on a job, and I'm just about to wrap it up," Roper said, "When I do, a lot of arrests are going to be made." He pointed at her. "You're one of them."

"Me?" she said. "Why would I be arrested? What for?"

"Sabotage, arson," Roper said, "maybe murder."

"Murder?" Her eyes widened. "I never murdered anybody."

"No?" he said. "So what *have* you been doing?"

"All I do is set men up to be rolled," she said. "Like I tried to do with you."

"And those two would've killed me," he said. "That would've made you guilty of murder."

"That's crazy."

"Besides," he said, "that's not even what I'm talking about. That's your sideline, just a little something to make some extra money."

"So?"

"So you're up to something else, Nancy," he said. "We both know that."

"I don't know what you're talkin'—"

"Why are you sleeping with Pete Orton?"

Her eyes widened again, and her nostrils flared.

"Wh-What? How do you know—"

"Somebody told you to sleep with him, didn't they?" Roper asked. "You're not the boss, Nancy."

"I'm—I'm nobody's boss," she said.

"I know," he said. "What I need to know is, who is your boss?"

She stood there staring at him, several times looking as if she was going to say something, but every time stopping.

"Come on, Nancy," he said. "You help me put away the brains of this operation, and I'll put in a good word for you with the law when they bring you to trial."

"To trial?"

"Or maybe you won't even have to go to trial. What do you think?"

"I can't . . . I need time."

"Don't take too long," he said. "Leave a message for me with the doorman at the Cattleman's Club." He hoped that if and when she did that, the doorman would be Lester.

She was staring at him and opened her mouth to say something when the door slammed open. A man in a suit entered, his hands empty. But his demeanor was of a man with a gun in his hand.

"What's going on, Nancy?" he asked. "Are you entertaining men in your room now?"

"No, Aaron," she said. "He was just leaving—"

Aaron Bonner held his hand out to silence her. Roper could see he had a gun under his jacket in a shoulder rig.

This was the guy. This was Nancy's boss.

"You the owner of this armpit?" Roper asked.

"I own the Bullshead," Bonner said. "What about it?"

"Your customers are getting rolled," Roper said. "You better do something about it or you're going to be out of business." Roper turned and looked at Nancy. "Remember what I told you. Keep your boys away from me. I don't roll easy."

"Yeah," she said, "okay."

Roper looked at Bonner.

"I don't know if you've got a piece of this or not," Roper said. "Either way, I'd clean house if I was you."

"Who are you?" Bonner demanded.

"Like I said," Roper answered, "a guy who doesn't roll easily."

He walked past Bonner and out of Nancy's room, hoping he hadn't made a mistake about her.

59

Bonner closed the door after Roper left, then faced Nancy.

"What was that about?"

"Like he said," she replied. "I gave him to Eddie, and Eddie had the wrong two guys try to roll him. It didn't work."

"Who was he?"

"Just some guy," she said. "He was flashing a roll in here the other night, so I gave him to Eddie."

Bonner studied her, then nodded.

"Look," he said, "I told you to forget about that stuff, didn't I?"

"Yes, but—"

"Tell Eddie you're done," he instructed her, "and if he doesn't like it, he can take it up with me. Or with Hoke Jessup."

At the mention of Jessup's name, Nancy went cold. Jessup was Bonner's pet killer. He was like a weapon that Bonner pointed, and when he pulled the trigger, somebody died.

"Y-Yes," she said, "okay."

"When are you seeing Orton again?"

"Um, tomorrow night."

He pointed his finger at her.

"You tell me every word he tells you, you hear?" Bonner said. "Don't go soft on me, Nancy. The money from this is going to set me up in a good place, and I'll take you with me."

"I ain't soft, Aaron," she said. "If you know anythin', you know that."

"Yeah," he said, "yeah, I know that."

He turned to walk to the door, stopped next to a sofa with a bunch of throw pillows on it. He picked up a pillow, took out this gun, and turned to face her.

"Aaron, no."

"Sorry, Nance," he said, "I can't take the chance." He held the pillow in front of his .32. It would muffle the shot enough so that it wouldn't be heard downstairs.

"B-But . . . why?" she asked.

"That was Roper who just walked out of here," he said, "and you never said a word."

He pulled the trigger once. Goose down floated into the air.

Downstairs nobody heard a thing. The music was playing loud. Badly, but loud.

Roper reached the saloon floor and started across the room. All around him men were drinking and laughing, grabbing at the girls going by, or hugging the ones sitting in their laps.

He was walking past one table when the girl, laughing loudly, turned her head and looked at him.

He recognized her right away. Even beneath all the paint she had on her face, her small breasts spilling out the top of her dress as the man holding her hugged her around the waist. And she recognized him, too, although she didn't show it.

"Goddamnit!" he said. He reached out and grabbed her arm, pulled her from the man's grasp.

"Hey, friend," the man yelled. "Get your own girl."

Another girl went by at that moment, so Roper grabbed her with his other hand, swung her into the man's lap.

"Have a ball!" he said.

He dragged Dol Bennett out the front door.

60

He slammed the door of his room and said, "Scrub that stuff off your face."

He had dragged her out of the Bullshead, into a cab, and all the way to his hotel. The clerk and several others watched him drag her across the lobby floor and up the stairs.

All the way she was sputtering, trying to talk, trying to explain, but he wouldn't listen. He was too angry.

She landed on the bed when he pushed her in, and now she stared at him. He grabbed a towel and tossed it to her.

"Wipe your face," he told her again.

"What's wrong with you, Roper?" she asked. "You blew my cover. Why would you do that? I never blew your cover, did I?"

"I told you to go home," he said, "not to get a job in a nest of vipers."

She wiped her face with the towel and said, "Don't be so dramatic, Roper."

Roper took off his hat and his jacket, set them aside, then rolled up his sleeves. He sat down in a wooden chair and stared at her.

"How long have you been working there?"

"Weeks," she said. "Since I walked away from you that night. You didn't see me the other times you were in there, but I saw you. And I respected your cover."

"What have you been doing, Dol?"

"Me? I've been watching, and listening, and learning," she said.

"And what have you learned from all that watching and listening?"

"You want me to tell you the results of my investigation?" she asked. "Because if I do, I think it might help you with yours. But . . ."

"But what?"

"But what if we worked together?" she went on. "I tell you what I know, and you tell me what you know. I bet with an exchange of information like that, we could close this whole mess out."

He stared at her while she finished cleaning her face and then tossed aside the now multicolored towel.

"What do you say?" she asked.

"What have you heard?" he asked.

"Are we agreed?" she asked.

"We are, but you go first."

"I'm going to take you at your word."

She stood up and adjusted her dress, which had become twisted by his dragging of her. Without her makeup, she looked like a little girl, which made the dress look ridiculous, especially the way it revealed her small breasts. But he supposed there were men who would find her appealing, particularly in a saloon.

"I was hired by Mr. Bonner himself," she said as if reading his mind. "He found me 'cute,' said I'd appeal to lots of his customers. He had Nancy dress me, and do my face until I learned to do it myself."

"I need something a little less personal, Dol."

"I heard enough to know that Mr. Bonner has a lot of other things going on in town, other than the Bullshead."

"Is he involved in Nancy's sidelines of rolling customers?"

"No," she said. "In fact, he told her to stop doing that, but she didn't listen. He wanted her to concentrate on something else."

"Sleeping with Pete Orton."

"So you know about that," she said. "I shoulda guessed. Yes, he wanted that to be her only concern."

"So he's involved in the sabotage of the stockyards."

"Yes."

"But he's not the boss."

"No," she said, "but he thinks he is."

"How do you know that?"

"Nancy," Dol said. "She doesn't know who the boss is, but she said once that Bonner's not, he only thinks he is."

"So you've never seen Bonner with anybody else, maybe discussing the stockyards?"

"Yes, but only Jessup."

"Jessup?"

"Hoke Jessup," she said. "He's Bonner's thug, does all his dirty work for him."

"Including murder?"

"I wouldn't be surprised, but I don't know for sure that Jessup ever killed anybody."

"Did you ever hear the name 'Henderson' mentioned?"

"He's the man who was killed in the pens? Yes, I heard him mentioned, but only in passing."

"He was another detective, Dol, hired before the Pinkertons."

"Oh," she said, "I'm sorry to hear that."

"Is that all you have?"

"Isn't that enough?"

"I knew most of that."

"You didn't know about Jessup."

"Men like Bonner always have a Jessup," he pointed out. "I need something concrete to lead me to the man in charge."

"Well, what do you have?"

"I've already told you Henderson was a detective, you know that Nancy was sleeping with Orton to get information . . . seems you know most of what I know, too."

She frowned. "That's not fair! You're not telling me anything."

"There's nothing to tell."

"Who are we working for?" she asked.

"We?"

"I'm still a Pinkerton."

"I thought you were fired."

"Well . . . they'll take me back after they learn how I helped you."

"Maybe," he said.

"Come on," she said, "you've got to tell me something I don't know."

"I'm working for the Cattleman's Club."

"That's vague. Exactly who?"

"Even if you were my partner, Dol," he said, "that's not something you need to know. That's between him and me."

She put her fists on her hips, looking for all the world like a little girl who had gotten into her mother's dressing room.

"So what do we do now?" she demanded.

"Nothing," he said. "You do nothing. Go back to your hotel."

"I have to go back to work."

"No, you don't."

"I'll get fired!"

"You're probably already fired for leaving."

"But the job is not done."

"Look," he said, "I've planted a seed there that I hope will bear fruit."

"What seed?"

"Nancy," Roper said. "I'm hoping she'll come to me with the information I need."

"She doesn't know anything."

"No," Roper said, "she's too smart not to know anything. She's got something. She's a woman who looks out for herself."

"How will she know where to contact you?" she asked. "I could go back and tell her we're working together—"

"You'll get yourself killed if you go back there!" he said. "I told her to leave me a message at the Cattleman's Club, with the doorman."

"Are you sure the message will get to you?"

"I hope it will," he said. He realized in that moment that Lester the doorman might be working for Brewster. And if Brewster was the man he was looking for, the man in charge . . .

"Okay," he said, "I may have made a mistake."

"You?" she asked, making her eyes wide. "The great Talbot Roper made a mistake?"

"Look," he said, "all I'm saying is maybe you should go back, just to give Nancy a message, and then get out."

She touched her face and said, "I'll have to do my makeup again."

"Listen to me," he said. He went to her and took her by the shoulders. "I just want you to go back there and tell Nancy what hotel I'm in, so she can send me a message here instead of the Club."

"And what if she sends somebody to kill you instead?" Dol asked. "What if she tells Mr. Bonner, and he sends Jessup?"

"If that happens," he said, "I'll be ready."

61

Bonner sat at his desk, waiting. When the door opened and Jessup walked in, he said, "It's about time!"

"I just got your message." Jessup was a tall, rangy man with an easy way of moving that men who were comfortable with themselves had. The thing Bonner liked about him was that he was unflappable in the face of any task.

"I've got a job for you."

"That's what I'm here for," Jessup said. "What job?"

"You've got to get rid of a body."

"Whose body?"

"Nancy."

"Nancy's dead?" Jessup asked with only mild interest. "That's too bad. I was hoping someday she and I . . . oh well, who killed her?"

"I did."

Jessup chuckled. "Couldn't you just have fired her?"

"Shut up," Bonner said. "She's in her room. Get rid of her."

"Anyplace in particular?"

"Someplace she won't be found."

Jessup shrugged and said, "You're the boss."

"That's right," Bonner said. "I am." He waved. "Go. And after that, I'll have another job for you, one that's more up your alley."

Jessup gave Bonner a cocky little salute and left the office.

The boss, Bonner thought. He wasn't the boss, not yet. But he would be. Oh yes, he would be, and soon.

Jessup strolled through the casino and up the stairs. He entered Nancy's room and stared down at her body. He'd thought one day he'd get her into bed, that she'd eventually stop rejecting him.

"Too bad," he said to the dead woman. He knelt down next to her, touched the skin of her shoulder, the upper slopes of her breasts. He'd always wanted to see her naked. Maybe, since he was alone with her, just a peek . . .

Dol reentered the saloon, hoping that no one had missed her. She'd tried to fix her hair and straighten her dress, had been unable to redo her makeup, but hoped nobody would notice.

She worked her way through the crowd, avoiding the groping hands, and went up the stairs. She made her way to Nancy's door, thought about knocking, then simply turned the doorknob and entered.

She stopped short when she saw Jessup leaning over Nancy, who was lying on the floor, bloody, with the top of her dress pulled down to her waist. Jessup's hands were on her breasts as he turned his head and looked up at Dol.

"Hello, Dol," he said.

By the next morning Roper still had not heard back from Dol on whether or not she'd delivered her message. Worried, he went down to the lobby.

"Any messages for me?" he asked the clerk.

"No, sir."

Damn, he thought. He never should have sent Dol back in there, but she'd been there for weeks. Maybe he just never gave her enough credit.

He took a few steps away from the front desk, trying to decide on his next move, when he saw Detectives Carradine and Cole enter the lobby.

"Just the man we're looking for," Carradine said.

"What can I do for you, Detectives?"

"We got some bad news for you," Cole said.

"What's that?"

"One of your suspects has turned up dead," Carradine said.

"Who's that?"

"Nancy Ransom."

"Jesus," Roper said, "how?"

"She was shot, and dumped where somebody thought she wouldn't be found."

"But somebody did," Cole said. "A drunk stumbled over them."

"Them?"

"Yeah," Carradine said, "there was another gal with her. This one was strangled."

"Who was that?"

"We don't know," Cole said. "Ain't identified her yet."

"What's she look like?"

Carradine shrugged. "Saloon girl, kinda small. Why?"

"Take me to her," Roper said. "I might know her."

"Okay," Cole said, "come on."

When they removed the sheet, Roper found himself looking down at Dol Bennett. Lying on a slab, she seemed even smaller and younger, looking like a broken doll.

"Know her?" Carradine asked.

"Yeah, I know her," Roper said. "Dorothea Bennett. She was a Pinkerton."

"This little girl?" Cole asked. "Jeez, who sent her in there?"

"I didn't send her in," Roper said, "but I sent her back in."

"What's that mean?" Carradine asked.

Roper explained who Dol was, how she'd followed him to Fort Worth, how he'd thought she'd gone home, but instead, she'd gone undercover in the Bullshead.

"I dragged her out of there last night, but then I sent her back."

"What for?" Carradine asked.

"To deliver a message to Nancy," Roper said, flicking a thumb at the other body.

"Come on," Carradine said, "let's get out of here and talk someplace else."

On the street, Carradine led the way to a small café, where they all ordered coffee, even though Roper would have preferred a strong whiskey.

"Tell us," Carradine said.

"I shook Nancy up last night," Roper said. "I thought I had her ready to talk, but Aaron Bonner walked in on us."

"More scum," Cole said.

"What did he catch you doing?" Carradine asked.

"Nothing," Roper said, "I made it seem like I was warning Nancy to stay away from me, to keep Eddie Parker away from me."

"You think Bonner was running her game of rolling customers?" Carradine asked.

"No," Roper said. "He knew about it, but I think he wanted her to stop."

"Or maybe he wanted a piece," Cole said.

"No," Roper said, "Bonner's working on something bigger."

"The stockyards thing?" Carradine asked.

"I think so. He's got a fella named Jessup working for him."

"Hoke Jessup," Carradine said. "For a while he was suspected of every murder that took place in Fort Worth, but then he sorta faded from sight."

"He's working for Bonner."

"That's probably why," Cole said. "We've suspected for a while that Bonner's up to something, we just haven't been able to pinpoint what."

"Bonner and Jessup," Carradine said. "We've never connected them."

"But Bonner still isn't the boss," Roper said. "Somebody else is pulling the strings, and I thought Nancy was going to tell me."

"And maybe Bonner thought so, too," Carradine said. "That's why he killed her, or had Jessup do it."

"And your girl walked in on them," Cole said.

"Probably," Roper said.

"Not your fault, Roper," Carradine said. "If she was a Pinkerton, she knew the risks."

"She was a kid," Roper said. "She should've gone home."

"Well," Carradine said, "we're going to go and have a talk with Bonner, and probably Jessup."

The two detectives stood up.

"You want to come along?" Cole asked.

"No," Roper said, "I'm going to finish my coffee."

They stared down at him, then shrugged and left. He obviously wanted to be alone.

62

Roper wasn't sure about his next move.

He couldn't believe Dol Bennett was dead. He could still see her in his room, with her little fists on her hips, glaring at him. He never should have sent her back in there.

The police were going to talk to Bonner and Jessup, and Roper had already talked with Eddie Parker, Louise Orton, and Nancy. With the murders of Nancy and Dol, he felt things had to be coming to a head. In fact, he himself might be next on the list.

He decided that a visit back to the Cattleman's Club was in order. He just wasn't sure who he was going to talk to when he got there, Kalish or Brewster.

He stood up, realized he had to pay for all the coffees as the two detectives had left no money behind. He shook his head, dropped some money onto the table, and left.

As he stepped down from his cab, he saw Cullen Brewster getting into a cab in front of him. He made a spur-of-the-moment decision.

"Never mind," he told the driver, "I'm not getting out. Follow that cab."

"Yes, sir."

They followed the cab through the streets of Fort Worth, which, at this time of the day, were fairly busy. At one point they got stuck behind a delivery cart.

"Don't lose him!" Roper shouted.

"Relax!" the driver called back. "I ain't gonna lose 'im."

And he didn't. Eventually, Brewster's cab pulled up in front of a brick house on a fairly affluent street.

"Stop back here," Roper said.

His cab pulled to a stop and they watched as Brewster paid his driver and went into the house, using a key.

"What do we do, Chief?" the cab driver asked.

"Let's just sit here awhile."

"As long as you're paying."

Roper handed the driver some money and asked, "Will that hold you?"

"For a while," the man said, putting the money in his pocket.

They sat for about ten minutes, watching the front of the house.

"Hey," the driver said.

"What?"

"What if whoever he's meeting was already inside?"

"If that's the case," Roper said, "I'm not sure he would've used the key."

Five more minutes.

"Are you followin' him to see if he's seein' your wife?"

"No," Roper said, "not my wife."

"Oh, somebody else's."

"Yes."

"Why don't you go up and peek in a window?" the man asked.

"This fella knows me," Roper said. "I wouldn't want him to see me."

"I could have a look," the driver said. "I know this row

of houses. There's a cobblestone alley in the back, lotsa windows."

Roper hesitated, then said, "That might be a good idea, but hurry back, in case he comes out."

"If he comes out," the driver said, stepping down, "go ahead and take the cab. I'll just meet you back here. My name's James."

"Okay, James," Roper said. "Thanks. If I have to take your cab, I'll double your fee."

"That works for me," James said.

James hurried down the street toward the building, then cut down an alley between buildings that Roper had not even spotted. After fifteen minutes no one had come out. But James the driver was coming back.

"He's in there alone, drinking."

"Drinking what?"

"Whiskey."

James climbed up into his seat.

"We still waitin'?"

"We're still waiting."

That's what Roper's business was about.

It took forty minutes from when they first arrived, but another cab pulled up in front of the house, and a woman got out. Roper leaned forward and narrowed his eyes.

"That her?" James asked. "That your friend's wife?"

"That's her."

They watched as she knocked, and then went inside. Roper got out of the cab.

"Show me," he said.

"Show you what?"

"Show me the window you looked through."

James hopped down and said, "Come on."

63

Brewster took the woman's wrap, tossed it on a chair, then took her by the shoulders, turned her, and kissed her. She gave him one kiss, but when he leaned in for another, she turned and walked away.

"I'd like a cigarette," Louise Orton said.

He took one out, lit it, and handed it to her. He watched her breathe the smoke in and out. She was an incredibly sexy woman. What she was doing with Pete Orton, he never understood.

"When is this going to be over?" she asked.

"Soon," he said. "The investors are coming in. When they hear about the fire, that'll be it. They'll pull out."

"And then?"

"And then my people come in."

"And then what?"

"And then you leave your husband and you come with me," Brewster said. "We'll have more money than everyone at the Cattleman's Club combined."

"You keep saying that," she said. "What about Roper?"

"What about him?" Brewster asked. "I'll have Jessup take care of him."

She shivered when she heard Jessup's name.

"And Nancy?"

"Nancy's been taken care of."

"By Jessup?"

"What difference does it make?" Brewster said. "She's gone."

"And Pete?"

"He'll be out of a job," Brewster said.

She drew on her cigarette again, her arms folded.

"Does that bother you?"

"I'll tell you what bothers me," she said. "That detective."

"Now that we know who he is, he'll be taken care of," Brewster said. "Just like the other one."

"This one's not like that other one."

"I know," Brewster said. "I knew there was something about him from the moment I met him."

"Then you should have taken care of him right away."

"Not until I was sure," Brewster said. "You see, darling, that's the secret of my success. I don't move until I'm sure."

"I wish I could be sure," she said.

Roper looked in the window, watched as Brewster took Louise Orton's wrap and kissed her, then watched as she turned away. She wasn't happy. But Roper was.

"Okay," he said, "you go back to your cab and wait for me."

"Where are you goin', boss?"

"I'm going to join the party," Roper said.

They went back down the alley to the street.

When the knock came at the door, Louise's eyes went wide.

"Who's that?"

"I don't know," Brewster said. "Nobody knows we're here."

"Don't answer it."

"Don't worry," he said, touching the gun beneath his arm. "Just wait here."

He walked to the front door and opened it.

"Hey," Roper said, "invite me in."

Brewster took only a moment to decide, then said, "Come in, Mr. Roper."

Roper followed Brewster into the room where Louise Orton was waiting.

"What's he doing here?" she demanded.

"Relax," Brewster told her. "Mr. Roper just wants to talk, isn't that right, Roper?"

"That's right, Brewster," Roper said. "Just a talk."

"And that's really all you can do, isn't it?" Brewster asked. "Because you can't prove a thing. Not legally."

"You're right," Roper said. "I can't prove that you've been behind all the sabotage, the fire, the murder of Walt Henderson—who, by the way, was a stock detective. But I'm here to tell you that doesn't matter."

"Is that a fact?" Brewster said. "And why is that?"

"Because I don't have to prove it to the law," Roper said. "That wasn't my job."

Now Brewster frowned, a bit confused.

"What was you job, then?"

"Just to find out who was behind it all," Roper said, "and I have. You."

"So what are you going to do now?" Louise asked.

"I'm going to leave," Roper said. "I just wanted you to know that I knew."

"That's it?" Louise asked. "Who are you going to tell?"

"Do you mean am I going to tell your husband about you and Brewster?"

"She doesn't care about that," Brewster said. "She's done with that loser anyway. No, she wants to know who you intend to tell about me."

"Just the people who hired me."

"And who was that?" Louise asked.

"The Pinkertons," Roper said. "What they do with the information is their business."

"Cullen," Louise gasped, dropping her cigarette, "kill him! You can't let him leave!"

Roper looked at Brewster, knew he had a gun beneath his arm.

"Go ahead, Brewster," Roper said, "pull that hogleg. Let's do it like the Old West."

There was a tense moment, and then Brewster slowly raised his hands and said, "Uh-uh. I'm not going to let you kill me."

"Kill him!" Louise yelled.

"Shut up, Louise!" Brewster shouted. "He can't prove a thing."

Roper backed toward the door so that Brewster was not tempted to shoot him in the back. As he went down the steps outside, a smile played about his mouth, because he knew all he had to do was tell the Pinkertons what he knew. They had their own bully boys for the rest of the job. Taking care of Brewster didn't have to be legal. It just had to be done.

64

Roper lied.

He didn't just tell the Pinkertons.

He told Harold Kalish at the Cattleman's Club.

"Sonofabitch," Kalish said.

It was early the next morning and Lester the doorman had shown Roper right in to see Kalish. He had already sent a telegram to William Pinkerton.

"Can we prove it?" Kalish asked.

"Not legally," Roper said, "and he knows that. Oh, I could probably work on it a lot longer, but I'm already on to something else."

"What's more important?" Kalish asked.

"Murder."

Kalish frowned. "Yes, I suppose it is."

"The Pinkertons will take care of Brewster," he said. "Or you could do it yourself."

"How?"

"Take away all his power," Roper said. "Get together with the others, and kick him out."

"That would . . . that would kill him," Kalish said.

"Yes, I know," Roper said. "With men like that, it's

always about power. Not having power, that's the worst thing for them."

"By God," Kalish said, "we'll do it." He extended his hand to Roper. "Thank you, sir."

Roper shook his hand and said, "Believe me, it was my pleasure."

"So I suppose you'll be leaving town?"

"In a couple of days," Roper said. "I still have a loose end or two to tie up."

His next stop was the law office of William Catlin.

"It's good to see you," Catlin said as Roper sat. The office was modest, to say the least, but that was okay. "You're looking prosperous, Andy."

"Not Andy," Roper said. "My name is Talbot Roper, and I'm about to do something that may lead me to need a lawyer. If I get caught."

"Then you came to the right place," Catlin said. "Tell me about it."

And he also told one other person.

Detective Cole joined Roper at the table in the small café where they'd last had coffee together.

"We've got nothing on Bonner for the murder of Nancy and the other girl," Cole said.

"What about Jessup?" Roper asked.

"Even less."

"Can't touch them, huh?"

"Nope. What about you, How's your case going?"

"I solved it."

"You did? Who's the guy?"

"Cullen Brewster."

Cole sat back in his chair and said, "The Cattleman's Club guy?"

"That's right."

"Sabotage, arson . . ."

". . . and murder."

"Just tell me what proof you got and I'll arrest him," Cole said.

"No legal proof," Roper said. "I just know he did it."

"Not by himself."

"No, I'm sure he used Bonner, and probably Jessup."

"But you've got nothing legal."

"Nope."

"Then I can't act."

"That's okay," Roper said. "Like I told Brewster, it wasn't my job to get him arrested, just to find out who was behind it all. And I did."

"And told the others at the Club?"

"I did."

"And the Pinkertons?"

"Yes."

"But . . . they'll kill him," Cole said. "The Pinkertons, I mean. They're not above . . . murder."

"No, they're not," Roper said, "but nobody can prove that."

"No, they can't," Cole said. "I guess nobody can prove anything."

"No."

"But somehow," Cole said, "I think it'll all get taken care of."

"Yes," Roper said. "It will."

Aaron Bonner closed the safe in his office and spun the dial. It had been a long day. The saloon was empty and everyone had gone home. As soon as he got his payoff from Brewster—and he, in turn, paid off Jessup—he'd have the money to open his new place, and it would put the White Elephant to shame.

He stood up, turned, and stopped short when he saw Roper.

"Wha—What the hell are you doing here?" he demanded.

He eyed the top drawer of his desk, where he'd just put his gun.

"We have unfinished business."

"We—what business do we have?"

"Nancy Ransom," Roper said, "and a girl named Dol."

"Dol?"

"You killed one or both of them. Whichever one you didn't kill, your man Jessup did."

Roper took out his gun.

"Wait, wait," Bonner said, "Jessup did it. He killed 'em both."

"On your order."

"Never," Bonner said, "I never—it was Brewster. See, he owns this place, not me. I'm just a front for him."

"But a man like you always has his own plans," Roper said. "At some point you'd double-cross Brewster, if you got the chance. Well, you're not going to get that chance."

Bonner was breathing so hard he was starting to hyperventilate. He clutched his chest, staggered, grabbed the edge of his desk, and then went for the drawer with the gun in it. He got it open, got his hand on the gun, and Roper—glad Bonner had made the attempt—shot him.

"No, no," Bonner said, slumping to the floor. "Not fair . . . not . . . I was gonna open a place . . . a new place . . ."

Roper stood over him and said, "No new place for you, Bonner," and shot him again.

Epilogue

Roper rode into Socorro on his rented horse. His saddle and horse were still back in Denver, where he had not yet returned. He had left Fort Worth when he realized Hoke Jessup had fled, for whatever reason. Maybe he thought the law would be after him after what happened to Bonner and Brewster.

Roper took to the trail, tracking Jessup, always a step or two behind him. But he finally got the word that Jessup was in Socorro. He only hoped he would still be there when he arrived.

It took him two days since the word had reached him. He had ridden day and night, because Dol Bennett deserved no less. The girl should never have died.

Socorro was like most border towns, with adobe buildings, dusty streets, both American and Mexican citizens. And people passing through, on the way from or to the United States.

He felt years older when he got off his horse in Socorro

in front of a cantina. He tied the horse off and went inside, ordered a cold *cerveza*.

He was halfway through the beer when a man wearing a badge sidled up next to him. He had a sombrero hanging behind his back and a badge on his chest that had no writing or etching on it. He was a portly man with a quick, ready smile which revealed teeth of silver, gold, and yellow.

"Welcome to Socorro, *señor*," the man said.

"Thank you."

"I am *el jefe* here, *señor*—how you say in your country— the sheriff."

"Good for you."

"May I ask, *señor*, why you are here?"

"Sure," Roper said, having no reason to lie, "I'm looking for a man. I've been looking for him for three months."

"Ah," the sheriff said, "*Señor* Jessup."

"That's right. Is he still here?"

"Still here, *señor*," the man said, "and very, very tired of running. He had been running from you, no?"

"I hope so."

"Well, he will run no more," the sheriff said.

"You have him in your jail?"

"Oh, no, *señor*," the sheriff said, "he has broken no law here. But he and I, we have become *simpatico*, we have talked."

"You made friends with him?" Roper asked, surprised.

"Well, I am a friendly man, *señor*," the lawman said. "What can I tell you?"

"You can tell me where he is."

"He is waiting, *señor*," the sheriff said. "He has been here waiting for perhaps a week."

"Where is he . . . exactly?"

"I will take you."

"And I will let you take me," Roper said, "but if this is an ambush—"

"*Señor*," the sheriff said reproachfully, "I would not take part in such a thing. And I do not take sides in the disputes of others. I am simply delivering a message,"

"All, right," Roper said, putting his beer mug on the bar. "Lead the way."

"*Sí, señor,*" the sheriff said. "Come with me. I will take you to him."

Roper left his horse in front of the cantina and followed the sheriff on foot. The portly man led him to the end of town, perhaps the very last building.

"He is in there, *señor.*"

"Doing what?"

"Drinking," the sheriff said, "preparing to kill, or be killed."

"Just like that?"

"*Señor,*" the sheriff said, "you have chased him for many months. A man, he becomes tired of running, no?"

"He becomes tired, yes," Roper said. "Now you deliver a message for me. Tell him I'm out here."

"*Sí, señor,*" the man said, "that was my intention."

The portly man hurried into the small, run-down building. Roper didn't know if it was a cantina, or somebody's house—he just cared that Jessup was inside. And that he was coming out. He was still wary, though, of a possible ambush.

The sheriff came hurrying out and said to Roper, "He is coming, *señor.* I wish you luck. I, uh, will stand aside, if you do not mind."

"I don't mind."

The sheriff hurried off to one side just as Jessup appeared in the doorway. He was a bleary-eyed, disheveled mess, and Roper knew he looked much the same.

"Roper," Jessup said.

"Jessup."

The killer stepped out into the open. He wore his gun low on his right hip. He had long arms.

"All this for some little saloon girl?" he asked. "You been doggin' me all this time—"

Roper drew and fired. His bullet hit Jessup in the chest

and the man's eyes went wide. His mouth opened, but no sound came out, and then he slumped to the ground. Roper was not a gunfighter; he wasn't a fast draw. Jessup might have been. Roper couldn't take the chance.

As he holstered his gun, the sheriff ran to Jessup, checked his body, then walked to Roper.

"You gave him no chance, *señor*."

"No," Roper said, "no chance at all."

He walked back to his horse.

Don't miss the best Westerns from Berkley

. . . .

LYLE BRANDT
PETER BRANDVOLD
JACK BALLAS
J. LEE BUTTS
JORY SHERMAN
DUSTY RICHARDS

. . . .

penguin.com